All Eyes On Tommy Gunz

PART FOUR

Warren Holloway

AMERICA'S NEW STORYTELLER

GOOD 2 GO PUBLISHING

ALL EYES ON GUNZ 4

Written by Warren Holloway

Cover Design: Davida Baldwin – Odd Ball Designs

Typesetter: Mychea

ISBN: 978-1-947340-30-5

Copyright © 2018 Good2Go Publishing

Published 2018 by Good2Go Publishing

7311 W. Glass Lane • Laveen, AZ 85339

www.good2gopublishing.com

https://twitter.com/good2gobooks

G2G@good2gopublishing.com

www.facebook.com/good2gopublishing

www.instagram.com/good2gopublishing

CHAPTER 1

A FEW DAYS after Tom "Tommy Guns" Anderson revealed to his mother that he was still alive, in California, Ramon, the man who had helped him escape prison and be declared dead, was in his multimillion-dollar mansion in a gated community. He was relaxing and being entertained by two exotic women from an escort service. While lying in his large California king-size bed, he loved how the ladies catered to his every need.

Ramon's security detail protected his house and its perimeter to the fullest. Additionally, he had cameras located throughout the house as well as outside that he could access and monitor with just a tap on an iPad screen.

The Asian beauty sucking his dick was like a porn star, humming on him to add sensation to her movements. The blonde kissing him was just as horny. The Asian beauty stopped sucking his dick only to mount him, which allowed her tight, wet pussy to slide down on him and make him feel just as good as she felt with his thick manhood inside of her. She worked her hips back and forth and up and down, slamming hard on his dick. She wanted it all up inside of her. At the same time, she could feel her tight pussy getting wetter and wetter while sliding up and down on his dick.

"Mmmmmmh, yes, yes! Ohhhhh!" she let out as her head went back while embracing the feeling.

Ramon loved what he was feeling with her tight pussy; but being a man of power, he stopped her in mid-ride.

"Switch! I want you to ride me now," he said to the blonde.

The Asian girl came off of his dick, licked her fluids off him, and kissed the head before passing him over to her girl.

"You going to like this dick, bitch!" the Asian girl said to her friend.

The white girl's pussy was already wet from playing with herself as she was watching them go at it. Her pussy felt deep to him, but he still thrust his hips and sent his dick inside her with power that made her moan as he went side to side and deeper and deeper. She also loved the feeling. She placed her hands on his chest and embraced the wave of sensation that was coming through her body, making her ride him with intensity.

"This feels good right here! Mmmmh, mmmmmh,

mmmmh, aaaah, aaaah, aaaah!" she let out.

She could feel her girl's fingers tweaking her nipples. At the same time, her friend used her other hand to thrust her fingers inside of her pussy, which made Ramon's dick feel even tighter inside of her wetness.

"Ohhhh! Ohhhh! Bitch this is good! Mmmm-mmmh, mmmmmh! Oh God, I'm cumming! Mmmmmh, ohhhh damn this feels good!" she let out, feeling the Asian beauty's fingers assist in her intense orgasmic pleasure that she felt rush through her body.

She was unable to stop and could not hold it back anymore as it came racing through.

"Aaah, aaaah, aaaaah, aaaah!" She started riding him and her girl's fingers harder and harder.

The orgasmic wave streaming through her body made her cum over and over, feeling like a swarm of orgasmic butterflies taking over her body. He also busted from hearing her moans, which stimulated him as she was going up and down, harder and faster on his dick. He could not hold back anymore. The Asian beauty pulled out her fingers from the blonde's wet pussy and licked them.

"I like your sweet taste, Roxi," the Asian beauty said as she leaned in to kiss her friend's breasts, nipples, and then up to her lips.

She did not resist, even though she had never been with a woman before. There was just something about the moment and her touch that stimulated her mind and body.

In the midst of all the fun, Ramon's business cell phone sounded off, bringing a halt to everything in the room.

"*Mira blanquita*, get off of me. I have to take this

call," he said, turning serious because business was always more important than pleasure.

He knew that good business was punctual and meant more money, and more money meant more power and respect.

"Speak! Time is money!" Ramon said, getting straight to the point.

"It's me, Nino. I want you to know that everything is official," he said while checking in just as Ramon had asked him to do.

"That's good. Check back with me when you're ready, hermano."

"Alright, I'ma holla at you then."

After the call, Ramon focused back on the two beauties in his bed. He wanted to feel more and see more.

"Let's take this to the shower where we can have

some more fun," Ramon said.

Each of the women loved the idea of this, so they walked to the shower and gave him a runway walk of seduction as he followed behind them. He wanted more of these two. They did just that in the dual showers which boasted massaging jets and rain features in the ceiling, which allowed all parties to get freaky and wet.

Once the shower action came to an end, they made their way back to the bed. Out of habit, Ramon tapped the iPad screen to check his cameras. He saw that all his men around the perimeter were down as were all the men inside of the house from what he could see.

Suddenly, someone slid from behind the door and drew his attention as well as that of the two women. They wanted to scream, but the man had his finger to his mouth signifying to them that he wanted them to be silent. They did just that upon seeing the silenced 9mm in his hand as well as the all-black fatigues he was wearing, which gave them a clear vision of who he was.

"The security system you have really isn't that foolproof," the voice from behind Ramon said.

Ramon immediately reached for the gun on his dresser to his left; but as he turned, he saw that there were two men instead of just the one who had spoken up on the other side of the walk-in closet. Each of the men pointed their weapons at him.

"I wouldn't recommend that if I were you. I think you're smart enough to know who we are, what we do, and who we represent," the operative said.

"I pay on time, so tell me why you are here!"

"Our mutual associates want to know who authorized you to use our resources to get Tom

Anderson out of jail and keep him alive?"

"Tom Anderson no longer exists to the American people. Everyone thinks he's dead!"

"Our associates believe that with him alive he can become a threat to you, which in turn is a threat to those we work for. You understand? He's a murdering menace and a liability that you have to get rid of before it's too late."

Ramon really liked Tommy Guns because he reminded him of how he used to be growing up in the hood on his rise to power. Ramon really appreciated Tommy's gangsta lifestyle and loyal way in which he played the game. He did not want to see Tommy Guns rot in jail or get the death penalty, so he used his resources.

"I'll take care of him myself as soon as possible. Now get the fuck out of my house!"

Both of the trained operatives came up on Ramon and took his gun. They popped out the clip and ejected the round from the chamber before tossing the gun on the bed with the women. They then left the home.

After they exited his room, Ramon looked into the hallway and saw all his men unconscious on the floor from the tranquilizer darts with which they were hit. His security was the best of the best, but they were no match for these elite operatives that moved in stealth mode.

Ramon's cocaine was being supplied by the agencies, or as some would say, the higher government. He knew that whatever they said needed to be taken care of, he would do without question—like calling up Tommy Guns and arranging a meeting.

"Tommy, my amigo. How's the free and alive life treating you?"

"It's feeling good so far. I just have to get some things back in order and life will be great."

"I need you to come back West as soon as you get a chance. We have something to go over out here that can't be discussed over the phone."

Tommy Guns detected a change in his voice since they talked a day or so ago, when he told him to stay far away for awhile. His hood instincts kicked in and gave him a negative vibe.

"I'm driving right now, so it'll be a few days before I head back that way."

"No problem, mi amigo. I'll see you then," Ramon said before hanging up the phone and then staring at it and thinking about what he had just done.

He knew it was betrayal in the worse way toward a thug or goon he embraced. He also knew it would not be difficult, since Tommy trusted him for giving him another chance at the free world.

Tommy continued driving down the highway and thinking about the call as well as the tone of Ramon's voice. It did not match up with his attempt to be sincere and welcoming as if he really needed to talk business.

Tommy drove to Atlanta. He felt the rush as he entered the city that he once embraced as his own with his homies he met here, including Fat Money, Ra Ra, Little D, Geez, and his baby momma, Candy.

He made his way over to her crib. As he drove over there, he saw all the young niggas out in the hoods getting money, chasing down broads, and living that life to the fullest. Life was to trap all day and play all night.

Tommy made it to her crib and sat out in front of her spot for a few minutes. He thought about the life they had together, and she did not even know he was still alive. How would she take it? What if she had a nigga up in there? He did not want to bring any heat or attention his way.

A few minutes passed by before he made his way up the steps and knocked on the door. When Candy came to the door and looked through the peephole and saw him standing there, she could not believe her eyes. At the same time, her heart and mind started racing. She was unable to process what she was seeing. Maybe it was the love she had for Tommy Guns that came to her when she saw that he was really alive.

"Oh my God! I can't believe this shit!" she said, pausing while still having her eyes glued to the peephole. "Who is it?" she asked, hoping he was who she saw.

"It's me, Tommy Guns, baby girl," he responded, laughing at the sound of her voice. He really missed her.

"It can't be you! You're supposed to be dead!" she yelled while opening the door.

He walked right in, and she shut the door behind him. Her eyes were glassy, but she soon realized this was indeed the man she loved. He was alive and well, right before her eyes.

"You know this shit ain't right. I thought they took you away from me and my son," she said, stepping in close to him before raising up on her toes to kiss and hug him.

She then took a step back and took in a visual look at him, appreciating his presence.

"Does my brother know you're alive?"

"Nah, and don't tell him over the phone neither. We'll link in due time."

"I haven't spoken to him since the summer. He

promised to stay in contact, but he's been so busy living in Mexico with his new girl."

"Where's my son at?"

"He's over at my mom's house. We can go get him if you want."

"Nah, we can handle that later. You ain't got no nigga in and out of here, do you?"

"Stop playing with me, nigga! You know I ain't never roll like that, especially now with my son. I can't be having different niggas around him."

"I asked because I need to trust you and this environment more than ever. If you want, we can move somewhere far away from here after I take care of some things. I have a new start, new life, and a new identity. Don't ask me how, because that's a long story in itself. The good thing about this new life is that I get to see yo' sexy ass again," he said as he pulled her closer to kiss her soft lips.

She did not resist because his lips made her flash back to the good times when he always made her feel special and good inside. His hands slid down her back and over the curves of her ass that he was cupping with both hands. He then picked her up in deep lust while kissing her and feeling the heat in their bodies rising. He walked her over to the couch, laid her down, and pulled off her Victoria Secret shorts to expose her pretty, perfect landing strip that commanded his attention. He took his pants off and came back in toward her love spot, placing a kiss on her landing strip and then her inner thigh as if teasing her. He then backed up to allow his tongue to taste her love pearl with his tongue, which made her squirm at the feeling that had been neglected for so long. His fingers came into play and entered her tightness. He could hear her sucking in pleasurable air while enjoying the feel of his touch. It had been awhile for him, too, since he had to lay low. His tongue started to pick up the pace, which sent a stimulating sensation soaring through her body as his fingers continued to thrust in and out of her wet pussy.

"Tommy, I missed this! Mmmmmh, mmmmh, mmmmmh!"

Her back arched as she felt the butterflies bounce around in her belly as the sensation continued to build intensely with each stroke of his fingers and tongue circling over her pearl. She opened her eyes and looked at him. She remembered this was just how he used to make her feel before. He was definitely alive and doing his thing, she thought.

"Ohhhh, Tommy! Ohhhhh, this is feeling so good! Ohhhhh" she moaned, allowing him to know he was doing her body good.

His fingers still worked their magic, which made her feel so good. The feeling that was building in her body was ready to be released, and she couldn't contain her sensation of pleasure anymore. It was coming. She could feel it racing through her heart, stomach, and legs. It was overwhelming her and reaching its peak. She could not hold back as she moaned and squirmed, trying to embrace the intense sensation of orgasmic pleasure.

"Aaaaaaah, aaaaah, mmmmmmmmh, I can't, I can't hold it back! I'm cumming! Mmmmmh, mmmmmmmh, mmmmmmmmh."

Her legs shook when the orgasm took over her body, escaping with a powerful force of pleasure that was pulsating with passion. He could feel her squirting on his tongue. Her sweet taste made him go even harder, pleasing her body while loving the taste of it.

"Ohhhh, ohhhhh! Mmmmmmmh, mmmmmmmh,
Okay, okay! Stop, I can't take it! Mmmmmmmh,
mmmmmmmh," she let out as her body started cumming
again and again from his finger and tongue play.

Her body was just as he had remembered it. Her
legs closed in on his head as she held him in place on
her pearl and pussy. The surging sensation streamed
from her body with intense pleasure and made her feel
better than ever.

"Oh, oh, oh, aaaaah, aaaah, aaaaah! Make love to
me. Mmmmmmmh, mmmmmmmh!" she moaned,
wanting his dick inside of her now.

He slowed his tongue play down to entertain her
body in every way. Her legs still shook even after he
stopped coming up to her and kissing her lips. She
loved her own sweet taste as well while kissing the

man that made her cum so much.

"Be nice. It's been awhile," she let out as he entered her long and strong with passion.

She immediately felt the sensation in his body just as she felt it in her own.

"Aaah, aaah, aaaah, aaah, aaah! Mmmmmh, mmmmh!" she moaned as she felt him go deep into her wet love spot, hitting each side deep with love and passion in each stroke while stimulating her heart as well as her body.

Her lips against his neck lightly sucked on him as the pleasure she was feeling intensified with each stroke. She could feel her belly tremble as the orgasmic wave was flowing over her body with power as it raced to escape.

"Tommy, Tommy, mmmmmmh! Baby, I love you. Mmmmmh, mmmmmh, mmmmmh, mmmmmh,

mmmmmh!"

Her moans were more in depth as she felt her body let go of the orgasm at the same time he was working his dick by going deeper and deeper with passion. Her moans also triggered his motion and movement that picked up faster and faster. He began to breathe heavy as he started to feel the intense climax of his soldiers charging through his body. He could not hold back if he tried. Each deep stroke made her moan, and her moans stimulated his rising peak to make him ready to bust. He went faster, deeper, and harder, and then he busted inside of her as she moaned. She held onto him with all of her love, never wanting him to ever leave again.

A few minutes passed before he pulled out and stood up naked. She looked at him with love in her eyes, thinking about how he just had put it down on her. They made love before, but this was magnified by the thoughts of him being dead and now alive. She held on to the thoughts of him never leaving again, so it made this lovemaking session very good.

"Damn, Candy! You still got the juicy love that makes a nigga bust crazy!" Tommy said, being funny.

"You stupid! You still got gifts with the tongue and fingers, plus my kitty cat loves your stick!" she said while rubbing her pussy. "What's in the bag?" she then asked, when she looked over at the bag he had set down by the door.

"This is the money I saved over the years from being in the game. I need to keep it here. I'm going to buy a big-ass crib on the low somewhere, so we can have the good life we deserve together," he said, which made her feel good about this. He took out one of the vacuum-sealed bags of money with $100,000 in it.

"Yo, Candy, grab me a knife so I can open this."

He watched her get up naked and walk into the kitchen. She looked sexy in the nude, with her smooth ass with curves of perfection.

Candy came back into the room with a butcher knife.

"Really? That big-ass knife! What, you think I'm going to carve a deer or something?"

"Shut up before I smack you with it," she joked as she handed it to him.

"That would be some fucked-up shit. I heard of being pussy whipped and pistol whipped, but if you slap a nigga with a knife, how the hell he going to explain that shit!" Tommy chuckled at the thought of it as he cut out the bag of money.

He took out two $10,000 blocks and handed them to Candy.

"I want you to mail this to my mom. There's twenty stacks, plus here's ten for you, so you can get your closet right with the latest winter fashions. Plus, make sure my buck got what he needs, too," he added.

He put the remaining $70,000 to the side for his travels, and he then took the bag of money downstairs in the basement and tucked it away. When he came back upstairs, he walked up to Candy and palmed her soft naked ass.

"I'll be back in a few days or so. When I come back, you can have all of my attention."

"Tommy!" she said in her soft, loving, and sensual voice as her eyes locked on his. "Please come back. I don't want to go through this again."

"I'm coming back to get some more of this," he said while squeezing her ass and making her feel good and smile at the same time. "For real, I'm good. I'll be back so we can get back on track with our life. Don't worry, Candy," he said before kissing her soft lips and feeling the love and passion.

He made his way out of the crib and then climbed into his whip. She stood in the doorway watching him. He looked up toward the house and nodded his head before he pulled off. Their emotional attraction never left them, even with the time they were apart. Now with the physical intimacy they just had before he left, it only made their connection stronger.

He also knew that Candy would not be on the time that Shari was on, so his money was secured. His only thought now was on Ramon and what his intentions were with wanting him to head out West so soon.

CHAPTER 2

BACK IN NORTH Carolina, Dollar was in his hood stuntin' hard in his G55 Mercedes truck. He was feeling himself since he got off fifty bricks already, which was a good look for him and Nino. Dollar was posted up and waiting on L-Geez and Nino so he could see what they wanted to get into tonight.

Nino came down the street in his H2 with the beats banging music from his nigga from his city DJ Large Flava's mix CD. Dollar parked in front of the pool hall/game room where all of the hustlas hung out. Dollar saw Nino come down the street, so he jumped out of his whip in all black that matched his truck, his neck on icy, and wrist on freeze, making it even colder for those watching.

L-Geez also came down the street from the other

direction with his music blaring Young Jeezy's new shit.

Once they all exited their whips, their presences alone attracted women from the hood who were looking on at their whips and swagga with all of their diamonds blinging. The hattas were also out lurking in the cut.

As always, Nino stood by looking at all of the people around, yet he kept the hattas at bay.

"Yo, where the little homie Pistol at?"

"He's in Miami doing numbers. Plus he came on this shawty he was telling me about, so he's having it his way."

"He down there boo loving?"

"Nah, Pistol got pussy whipped," Dollar said jokingly, until the conversation turned to business when Nino started speaking.

"So what's good out here? We looking good on moving the work, or what?"

"I'm done with what you gave me," Dollar said after moving fifty bricks at 14.5, thanks to Nino looking out for him and allowing him to sell the bricks for 17.5 to 20 depending on who and where he sold them.

"Did you make ya money off of it?" Nino asked, making sure everybody was eating.

"You all ready? I got mine from the rip."

"L-Geez, what about you, my nigga?"

"I'm done too. We have to expand further now. Just think, the average city can do fifty to one hundred kilos a week, depending on the size of the city and its demand," L-Geez responded.

"Say no more. We'll work that out with the flow of product. The last fifty I'ma let y'all split that shit so we all can eat. One of y'all hit up Pistol to see what he's doing and where his numbers are. We can probably head back out West to see main man if Pistol's ready."

Nino made a total of $3.7 million thus far not counting the money he'd get from the fifty kilos he just gave L-Geez and Dollar to split. This flow of cash was only the beginning of a bright future dealing with the nigga Ramon, who was going to love seeing Nino's fast flow of the cash. The bags of money to Ramon were better than sex. This money and power shit turned him on.

Pistol picked up his phone on the second ring when he saw that it was the niggas he grew up with calling.

"What it do, folk?" Pistol answered his phone.

"We living that life getting to it. We need your numbers around here, so we can get it popping," L-Geez said.

"I'll be through tomorrow. I have to secure one more thing."

"Betta not be that pussy you securing!" L-Geez joked.

"Nah, nigga, I'm on my money chasing, folk."

29

"See ya when ya get here then," L-Geez said before hanging up the phone and making the crew aware of what he said.

Nino arranged for them to grab the fifty bricks plus the money they had for him.

They all met up a few hours later at Nino's townhouse with a few bad white bitches that gravitated toward them because they said they looked like rappers with all of the diamonds and tricked-out trucks. The women really embraced all of the bottles of Moët, Cîroc, and Rosé being circulated around the room, seeing these ballas living it up for real. Bottles of Hennessy were being poured to make the mood in the room light as everyone was feeling the buzz from the alcohol.

The one blonde favored a young Coco with baby-blue eyes and a golden tan. The other had body like Serena, with a tight stomach that was exposed under the red shirt she was wearing. It flowed with the body-fitting blue Prada jeans. Her green eyes were just as captivating as her thick-ass thighs and ass.

Nino was on the couch calling up Ramon when the thick, green-eyed white girl came over to him and unzipped his pants. She pulled out his dick and took it into her mouth. She looked into his eyes as her green eyes filled with lust as she began to please him.

"Damn, baby girl, you doing ya thing!" Nino said as her warm, soft, and wet lips slid over him and made him feel good.

"*Que pasa, mi amigo?*" Ramon said after answering the phone. Nino was still looking down at the white girl working her magic as he continued the call.

"Life is good. Business is better, my man."

"That's always good to hear. I take it we'll see each other soon?"

"In a day or so. I'll call you when I land."

"*Es tambien, hermano.* I'll see you then."

31

He hung up the phone feeling the sensation rushing through his body as her soft hand assisted in stroking him up and down as her mouth also went up and down, which stimulated him even more.

"Mmmmmmh, mmmmmh!" she moaned, vibrating her tongue and lips over his dick to make him reach his peak and not be able to hold it back.

"Damn, baby girl, here it comes!" he said while looking into her eyes as she continued pumping and sucking on him.

He could not hold it back anymore and exploded into her mouth of warmth. She continued to pump and suck, taking all of his flowing juice into her mouth and swallowing the last drop. She continued to squeeze and pump, still looking into his eyes while full of lust. She pulled out his dick, licked the head, and then kissed it before getting up.

"I swallow so I make memories and not a mess," she said, sitting beside him and pouring herself a double shot of Cîroc and then chasing down his juice with it.

"You a beast, blondy. I'ma definitely have to keep ya number locked into my phone," he said, making her laugh even though he was serious.

"Yeah, we rich, nigga! We changed the game around here!" Nino said to his homies.

Dollar stood up with a double shot of Hennessy in his cup. He was feeling himself getting all the money.

"I toast to my nigga Nino, for showing us all love and allowing us to get this fucking money!" Dollar announced before drinking his double shot.

Nino grabbed the remote to the sound system and turned on the classic Young Jeezy album *Thug Motivation*. As the tracks played, they were all feeling the getting-money music that inspired a true hustla to go get it.

"This is that getting-money music right here, boy!" L-Geez said while feeling the music and himself.

"If you listening to Jeezy and you getting this paper, then you in the way, ya hear me," Dollar said, flowing with the music and white bitches as the blue-eyed Coco lookalike started backing it up on him.

As they were all living it up and having fun, Tommy Guns was on the highway thinking about his plans to meet Ramon. He was so deep in thought that he did not even realize his foot was mashing the gas until a state trooper jumped out behind him flashing red and blue lights to get his attention. Immediately, the adrenaline pumped into his heart as his mind started racing and thinking about coming face-to-face with a cop. He pulled over and at the same time took hold of his new fully loaded nickel-plated .45 Desert Eagle ready to go with the laser beam on it.

Tommy didn't go into panic mode yet, because he had fake credentials that he took out of the glove box before the trooper got to his car.

The trooper came up with the flashlight out and

aimed it in Tommy's face, which blinded him a bit.

"You know what I pulled you over for, right?"

Tommy played stupid while at the same time started to speak real proper. He looked studious with his wire-framed glasses as he took the role of the person on his ID, a twenty-seven-year-old student at the University of Howard who was studying criminology and social behavior. He handed both forms of identification to the trooper.

"Son, you handed me your school ID, too," the officer said, handing it back to him.

It was Tommy's way of throwing him off a little, yet planting the seed of him being a college kid.

"Oh, I'm sorry, sir. I didn't realize it was mixed in there."

"Now, son, I pulled you over because you were clocked going fifteen miles over the speed limit."

"I'm sorry, I didn't notice."

Tommy was really into his character, playing the

role to the fullest to deceive the trooper. Contact with police was exactly what the agencies warned Ramon about. It was not good for continuous business. The trooper headed back to his car to run a check on the car that Tommy was driving as well as to check the identification and name for warrants. As he waited for the dispatcher to get back to him, he continued looking at the picture of Tommy Guns.

"Michael Mitchell, you look very familiar," he said to himself.

Then it came to him as the dispatcher returned over the radio to confirm the information on the ID. He made his way back to the car where Tommy Guns awaited with his hand on the .45 Desert Eagle.

"Mr. Mitchell, have you ever been on TV?" the trooper asked while looking at him with the flashlight, going back and forth from the ID to Tommy's face.

"Ah, no sir."

"Are you sure?" he asked again, making Tommy

feel anxious and ready to start shooting as his grip tightened on the .45 Desert Eagle ready to blast this muthafucka.

"I'm sure."

"I asked because you look like this rapper that's always on the BET station my daughter watches all of the time."

"That's the first I've heard that one," Tommy said laughing.

"All right, son, here's your ID. Drive safe."

Tommy pulled off and thought what a stupid muthafucka the officer was to possibly end his life and career because of his curiosity.

He focused back on driving with his plans to meet Ramon, but first he would make another trip to take care of business.

CHAPTER 3

DOWN IN MIAMI, Pistol, Raven, Diamond, and Tre were all over Tre's crib getting ready to step out to the clubs. Tre was still young and seventeen, but his swagga and money allowed him to get into a lot of clubs. Tre wore his stunna gear of a baby-blue sweat suit by Roc-A-Wear, baby-blue Air Force Ones, Sean Jean stunna shades, and a diamond tag with RIP Tommy Guns on it. The other tags had the names of Little D and Geez on them. Tre definitely was in stunt mode.

Pistol also wore the latest YSL attire bling on his wrist and in his mouth. He looked the part of a young king in the game.

Raven and Diamond outshined them both with their hair and nails done and their body and clothing on ten. They were also wearing the newest shit off the runway by Dolce & Gabbana.

Once they left the crib and headed to the club, each of them focused on a good time for the night. As Tre pulled up to the club, he saw his homie Trigger parking his pearl-white LS450 Lexus with 23s on it. Tre blew the horn to get his attention while at the same time he hit the switch on the BMW and rolled down his windows.

"Yo, Trigger, you up in here tonight, huh?"

"You all ready? I'm club hopping to see where the party's at."

"Say no more. The party is wherever we are, my nigga."

He parked his car beside Trigger's and then exited with Raven. Pistol also parked his truck before he and Diamond got out. Pistol was about to leave his gun in the truck until Tre raised his shirt up and displayed his 9mm Beretta, so he turned back, grabbed his gun, and tucked it into his waistline.

"Yo, the security going to let us ride with our straps?"

"They already know what we do, and that we'll shut this bitch down if they act funny," Tre said, walking past the two lines of people and up to the six-foot six security guard who already knew he was. He handed him $500 for the crew and VIP entrance. "I got another nickel for ya if ya get me into a suite."

The security did just that, after calling in over the radio to secure them a raised floor suite that was six feet off of the dance floor. It allowed Tre and his crew to view everyone on the floor; as well, being in the suite made them feel good and appreciated for their hustle and hard work.

The server entered the VIP suite and walked over to them.

"What y'all gentlemen having tonight?" she asked, looking good and the part of the Miami hostess life.

She had model features with dark, silky black hair,

gray eyes, and a golden tan that made her eyes glow even more. Her smile was as welcoming as her presence, which allowed her to make plenty of tips.

"Give us bottles of Patron, Cîroc, Hennessy, and Moët, and a few mixed drinks for the ladies," Tre said.

"My name is Amber. Anything you need tonight, and I'll be more than glad to help you with it," she said, working her hospitality to earn her tips for the night.

As she walked away, Diamond and Raven were checking her out.

"That sexy bitch better stay away from my man before I change her makeup and smack her around," Raven said while Diamond laughed.

"You know she's going extra to get her tips!" Diamond said.

"Just as long as she don't touch neither of our men."

Trigger didn't mind the attention of Amber whether she was working for tips or not. He appreciated her presence, because it was all a part of the VIP experience.

Amber came back within a few minutes, sparklers burning and lights blinking as her and a few other girls carried all of the bottles they ordered. All of the attention shifted to their VIP section, which allowed everyone to know where the young kings were.

"Here are your bottles. I also brought an orange juice and vodka as well as apple martinis. I'll set them over there on the table. We have food if you would like to order anything," Amber said, eyeing Tre and Pistol up and down, checking to see if the two of them were too young to be legally allowed in there, but wealthy enough to pay their way. She was obviously going to work her looks for tips.

As she awaited their response, she put her hand through her hair while giving each of them back-and-forth eye contact. At the same time, she lightly bit her bottom lip in a seductive manner. Trigger also saw this, so he stepped in because he wanted her attention as well.

"Pretty girl, bring fries and wings for the crew, along with them mini sliders, alright? Ya number would be fine, too, because my niggas are already taken, unless you like their girlfriends and shit," Trigger said.

Amber smiled at both of the girls as if to work them as well. She did not mind going both ways if she had to.

"That shit don't fly over here, mami! We only do dick. You pretty though," Raven said after giving her a brief smirk before the get-the-fuck–out-of-here look followed.

Amber took the hint and left the VIP area to put in Trigger's order.

Everyone was feeling good as they partied and enjoyed themselves, all toasting to the good life. Raven and Tre embraced their time and memories together, just as Diamond and Pistol did.

Tre raised his glass and spoke: "This is to my nigga Pistol for showing love to me and my city. To success and the good life!"

They raised their glasses at the same time while Raven looked on at her man. She wanted him sexually as always.

"To a good night, papi!" she said, pouring back her apple martini and then kissing his lips.

She allowed him to savor the flavor of the apple martini on her lips and tongue as they continued kissing with passion. She was so turned on that she would have let him take her right here if they were alone in the suite.

"I can't wait until we get home, papi," she said, giving him a look of seduction.

"I see you got a hot one there, Tre," Pistol said, seeing how Raven was being sexual toward him.

"Yeah, she likes to fuck."

"Only you, papi! *Mi amor es solo para ti*," Raven said while sipping her drink.

"On that note, my nigga, I'm going down to the dance floor," Pistol said, taking Diamond's hand and heading to the floor.

They mingled into the crowd and found their space, where they danced song after song. While breaking a light sweat, they also felt a buzz from the drinks they knocked back. Tre was still in the suite looking down at Pistol dancing with his cousin, Diamond. Pistol turned and saw him, so he raised his glass feeling the getting-money shit. Just then, a nigga bumped into him on the dance floor and then turned around as if Pistol had bumped into him.

"Yo, nigga, watch yo'self! You see me out here on the floor doing my thing!" the nigga said, eyeing Pistol up and down like he really wanted beef.

He had no idea that Pistol was strapped and would leave him on the dance floor. Diamond saw the murderous fire in her man's eyes, so she tugged on his arm to get his attention.

"Come on, baby, let's finish dancing. Don't pay this fool any mind. We didn't come here for that tonight," Diamond said, trying to calm him down.

He turned and looked into her eyes and then calmed down after seeing the fear in her eyes. They continued dancing for a few more songs; however, Pistol was watching his back in case the nigga really wanted beef with him and tried some lame-ass shit.

"I'm done dancing for now, baby. I'm going back to the suite to get a drink and some food," Diamond said. "You good out here by yourself?"

"I'm good, Diamond. I want to see more of the club. I'll be up," he said before kissing her glossy lips, which tasted like Peach Cîroc and vanilla lip gloss.

She headed back to the suite and left him to roam the club. He checked out all of the ballas and saw some potential clientele for himself or through Tre. Either way, he was always thinking about making money.

As Pistol was walking through the club, he saw many women and ballas. He then came across a sexy, caramel-brown-skinned sista who stood five foot two and weighed 125 pounds of thickness in her thighs and ass. She had a flat stomach she had exposed with the short shirt that showed off her diamond belly ring. She wore Gucci blue jeans and a tight white Gucci T-shirt with the logo and imprint. She had a short haircut that was close on the sides and curly on the top, which made her look even more exotic and model-like. She was a true Miami diva/go-getta. She noticed his eyes locked onto her.

"What's up, daddy? You looking real cute and fly. I know you're not from around here. Your whole swag is different."

"You right, shawty," Pistol said, looking around. "What's yo name?"

"They call me Hazel because of my green eyes that

change a little depending on my mood," she said, flirting with him and giving him the "you fine" look.

"I ain't gonna lie, shawty. You is fine, but I got a lot going on right now. But you best believe if I didn't, you would have all my time and attention," he said, getting a smile from her as she received his compliment and rejection at the same time.

She still wanted to give him her number just in case he became freed up from whatever he had going on.

"Yo, nigga, first you bump into me on the dance floor and now you trying to holla at my baby momma!"

"Chris! We are not together anymore, so who I talk to is my business!" Hazel snapped after feeling disrespected by him.

"Oh, so you want to fuck with this out-of-town nigga, huh?" he said, eyeing Pistol before walking away pissed off.

"Aye, shawty, you fine, but you need to put yo'

baby daddy in check."

"I'm sorry. Don't worry about him. I still want you to have my number if you feel like calling me," she said after giving him the number. He programmed it in, and then she leaned in and kissed him on the cheek and added, "I'll make it worth your while, whenever you decide to call."

Pistol was now intrigued and almost forgot about Diamond. He was captivated by Hazel's hazel eyes and also caught up by her natural beauty.

"I gotta go, shawty, but I might holla at ya sometime," he told her with a smile while walking away.

He then shifted to the more serious side of things as he made his way back up to the suite and over to Tre, who was still overlooking the dance floor.

"Yo, that nigga that bumped into you on the floor wants beef?" Tre asked.

"I don't think he wants that type of problem, ya

feel me?"

"These niggas is different down here in Miami. Don't lose focus or get caught up in the web, because that shit will backfire on you," he said, now referring to him speaking with Hazel.

"If Diamond would have seen this, she would have been pissed and probably beaten Hazel's ass. You see, I only fuck with Raven, because she's about me, and we going to ride this thing out until the wheels fall off."

Raven walked up on the two of them in mid-conversation.

"Papi, you talking about me?"

They looked at each other, and he noticed how her womanly instincts told her that this man she loved with her all heart was having words about her.

"Good things, mami! Only good things."

"You better not be talking bad things about me as much as I love you and ride for you," she said, caressing his back with one hand and holding a drink in the other.

"He's talking about how you make him a happy man, and he doesn't need anyone else because you're more than enough," Pistol said, helping Tre secure her all the way.

"Awww, papi! You really said that?" she said before leaning in to kiss him. "I love you, too, and you're all I need to make me and my body feel good," she added while nibbling on his ear.

He smiled from feeling her affection.

The night continued on until closing when the entire front of the club and parking lot looked like an after-party with all of the food vendor trucks and music blaring from multiple cars. As they exited the club and approached their whips, the nigga Chris came out of nowhere drunk and shouting.

"Yo, nigga, you think you the shit, huh!"

The entire crew turned fast toward the shouting

voice of the drunk-ass nigga. Pistol recognized the voice from inside the club. At the same time, each of them turned around to see who the fuck it was that they were taking out their weapons ready to roll on. Right then, gunfire erupted, which sent slugs through the air. Diamond caught a slug that slammed into her small frame, thrusting her back as the slug hit above her breast.

"Aaggggh!" she let out feeling the pain.

Pistol briefly looked at his woman being thrown back and became angered. He fired off multiple shots and gunned down Chris, before he took cover behind the cars, since the two niggas he came with were also strapped and popping back at them.

Raven jumped up from behind the car and unleashed her twin .380s, firing off multiple rounds and dropping the two shooters, killing one and wounding the other. The crowd of people dispersed, obviously fearing being shot. At the same time, they did not want to be witnesses in case guns were turned on them.

"Toma! Toma! I'll kill all of you puntas for shooting my homegirl!" Raven snapped as she emptied her weapons. She thought both of the shooters were dead as she stood over top of them and turned to speak to Tre. "I got these cabrons, papi!"

Raven was so caught up in the moment that she did not see the wounded shooter reach for the gun that got knocked out of his hand when she shot him. He was only inches away as he reached out to grab his gun and shoot her. He got ahold of the gun, but at the same time, Tre saw his movement. He charged in Raven's direction and yelled out, "Raven! Watch out!" He squeezed the trigger on his 9mm and sent five slugs through the air, just in time to bring a halt to the nigga's movement.

Two of the five slugs found their target and sucked the life from his flesh, forcing him to drop the gun.

Raven turned around and realized that she had almost been killed. She then took hold of Tre's gun and fired off a few more rounds into the nigga's body out of anger.

"Yo, let's go! Them boys is coming!" Trigger yelled out while jumping into his Lexus and taking off.

Pistol put Diamond in his truck before following Tre and Raven to the hospital to get his girl some medical attention.

CHAPTER 4

BACK IN HARRISBURG, at 11:01 the next morning, Agent Miles sat at the dining room table in his home. He was loading his standard-issued 9mm with hollow-point rounds in between downing shots of tequila. He was in a state of ignominy as if he had let down his family and co-workers. His family still had not been returned to him. The pain he was feeling was unbearable, in that he was unable to have what he loved the most: his family and job. He kissed the photo he had of his wife and daughter in between shots. He was getting drunker and drunker, after he had already downed half of the fifth that was sitting in front of him. He held the picture of his wife in his hand while tears filled his eyes.

"I'm sorry, Deborah, but I can't go on without you and my baby girl."

He placed the photo on the table in front of him.

He took another shot of tequila before picking up the

9mm, chambering a round, and placing it to his temple.

He then closed his eyes as if to embrace what was to

come.

"Daddy, what are you doing?" his daughter asked

while standing at the edge of the dining room with her

mother, who became speechless upon seeing her

husband holding a gun to his head.

Agent Miles opened his eyes and wiped them clear

as he turned toward the voice of his daughter and saw

her looking at him with innocent eyes. His wife with

also now crying; however, at the same time, she was

glad that she was able to make it home in time before

he had killed himself. He stood up and rushed over to

embrace his wife and daughter.

"I'm sorry I couldn't protect you from those

people."

"It's not your fault, honey. You did what you could."

"They forced me to retire because of the investigation I was leading to expose them."

"It's okay, Jason. We can move somewhere far away and figure this all out. I don't want our daughter to have to go through this again," she said before pausing and looking over at the gun on the table, realizing how close she was to losing her husband. "Baby put that gun away, please."

He turned to put the gun away, just as the doorbell rang followed by a knock on the front door.

"I'll get it, Jason," she said, wanting him to put the gun away.

"No, I'll get it; because if it's someone here to hurt me, I don't want them getting to you or Kayla," he said, grabbing the gun from the table and making his way to the front door.

He was feeling a little tipsy from all the tequila he'd had to drink. As soon as he opened the door, he sobered up as much as possible when he saw that it was director Mike Davenport with close to a dozen Federal agents with him for support.

"Agent Miles, are you okay? Did you get your family back?"

"Yes, sir! They just came in, which makes me okay, too," Mike said as he walked back inside and over to Deborah.

"Ma'am, I'm sorry all of this took place. We'll get to the bottom of this," the director said, handing her an envelope. "This is a letter from my superiors that is unaddressed with no signature. But just know that I speak on their behalf of the people that are behind your husband and myself. We are truly apologetic."

After he was done speaking, he shook her hand and then turned to Jason and embraced him to get close and whisper, "Your house is wired for sound, and they're watching you. Read the letter that I gave your wife for further instructions."

When Agent Miles heard this, his heart started racing, which sobered him up in seconds. He wanted to be alert for his family.

"I think I'll be going now. Take care of yourself, Agent Miles. It was nice having you at the bureau."

As soon as they left, Agent Miles took his wife and daughter upstairs. Once they reached the top of the steps, he whispered and made her aware of the audio and video from the same people that had taken her and his daughter. He started reading the letter that was not an apology; instead, it was intel on everything they had been searching for. He finished reading the letter and tucked it into his pocket. He knew that he would have to keep it close to him at all times. He was back in play; however, the people watching him could not know this. So he would approach everything discreetly, thinking ahead of those listening and watching his every move.

CHAPTER 5

DOWN IN MIAMI, Tommy Guns was just waking up in his hotel suite. After he got himself together, he headed out to his whip, certainly appreciating the Miami winter with the sun being out. He drove over to the projects where he once laid his head with Kiss, the exotic dancer, and over to Tre's crib.

When he pulled up to the projects, all of the young bucks hustling thought he was a fiend in the car he was driving, plus they did not know who he was. He parked the car and got out as the young hustlas ran up to him.

"What you need? We got nicks, dimes, twenties. Whatever you got money fo', we got ya!"

Tommy started laughing at the young niggas not recognizing who the fuck they were talking to.

"I'm good, little niggas. That's not my thing."

Tommy was looking like new money with his clothes, but they didn't match his down-low car that he was driving. All his clothes were new, but he didn't wear any diamonds because he did not want to attract any attention.

He made his way over to Tre's old crib; however, he was unaware that he no longer lived there. As he stood there knocking on the door, the young niggas in the hood wondered why he was at the stash spot, so they called up Tre.

"Yo, Tre, this nigga's knocking on the stash house door."

"Everybody in the hood knows what it's hittin fo', so this nigga must not be from around here," Tre said.

"I'm a few blocks away, so make sure he don't go anywhere."

"Alright, my nigga!"

Tommy knocked one more time as he was looking around, wondering if he would see Tre in the hood trapping, but he wasn't around.

"Who you looking for, folk?"

Tommy Guns turned around and saw that there were a few young bucks coming his way as if they were ready to get at him.

"I'm looking for my little homie."

"Nobody lives there anymore."

"Good looking, little nigga," he said while walking back to his car.

As he rushed the door of his car, one of the young bucks yelled out, "You look like 5-0!"

He viewed this as disrespect. He wanted to turn around and slap the shit out of the young buck.

"Little niggas, if you knew who the fuck you were talking to, you would show me a lot more respect!"

"Fuck you, nigga! You come into this hood again, we going to lay you out!"

Tommy had his hand on the door handle and was reaching for his .45 Desert Eagle, when a voice came from behind him.

"I wouldn't do that if I were you. Just get in the car and leave while you still can."

Tommy was pissed and gritted his teeth. He wondered who the fuck was telling him to keep moving. When he turned around, he saw a gun pointed back at him. It was his little homie, Tre.

"Lower that gun, nigga! You don't recognize who you're pointing it at?"

Tre looked shocked for a brief moment.

"Oh shit, this nigga done faked his death. Tommy Guns, my muthafucking old head," Tre said as he got out of his car.

"Yeah, nigga, it's me!"

"How the fuck you pull this shit off? You on some Machiavelli shit?" he said as he stepped up to embrace Tommy Guns. Then he looked at his whip. "Oh, you staying real low up in that joint."

"Yo, I heard the homies Little D and Geez got hit up."

"That nigga Tony the Ghost had his team do that shit. They came for me, but you know we stay ready in this hood," Tre said, hyped to see his old head. "Plus, the fiends had a field day taking them bodies out of the hood."

"You a real nigga, Tre. I see them tags you rocking."

"Papi, show him the tattoo," Raven said from the front seat.

Tommy was impressed by his loyalty, even after

he thought he was dead.

"I really fucks with you, little nigga. You as real as it gets, next to me, of course," he said.

Tre embraced it all, knowing it was coming from the real OG. The young niggas in the hood now realized who it was they were talking to, so they came up and apologized.

"Yo, my bad, OG. We didn't know that it was you. You know we just holding it down for the homie, Tre."

"Y'all good," Tommy Guns said after checking out how Tre had grown in age and business. "I see you grabbed the big boy BMW, too. It's a good look for you."

"Wait 'til you see the crib I got for me and my mom!"

"A new spot, huh?"

"Yeah, I dropped $250,000 on that spot, so me and

mom can live right."

"You deserve it. Tell ya mom I asked about her. I know she'll trip off of me being around."

"Did you tell Ra Ra about you being alive?"

"I will, but not over the line, feel me?" he said before he pulled Tre to the side to make him aware of what was going on. "Yo, the nigga who faked my death is down with some powerful muthafuckas on some heavy in-the-game shit. They got some serious connections, especially doing what they did to keep me around."

"Damn, OG! This is some mafia movie shit!" Tre said before getting back to business. "I still got yo' bread, too! I wasn't giving it to that nigga Tony."

"Good looking, my nigga. Get it to me when you can. I got plans for us. Right now I need you and your team to rock out with me on something out West, but they have to be on point to make this shit go right."

"Just let me know what it is, and I'll put them on to it."

"The people I just told you about may have a change of plans for me, so I want to make sure I stick around, ya feel me?"

"I'm with you, OG, and my team is with me. So we got ya!"

"Don't worry about guns; I got all that in check already."

"Fo' you, my nigga, we ready now. It's good to see you breathing; and now that you're back, we going to get it done. After we take care of this shit, we'll take a much-needed vacation."

Tommy laughed when thinking to himself that would be a good idea.

"Let's go to my crib so I can show you how I

stepped it up. Yo, Raven, we riding out, mami," he said while stepping into his BMW.

Tommy followed behind them in his whip and drove off. As they were driving through the projects, they saw a fiend snatching a young nigga's work and then taking off running until he was gunned down. Tommy was tripping seeing that these little niggas were holding it down just as Tre would have if he was running around himself.

CHAPTER 6

BACK UP IN North Carolina, Pistol, Nino, Dollar, and L-Geez were all at the stash house counting all of the money they would take out West to secure the shipment of more cocaine.

"I got to get Ramon 1.8. I'll grab two hundred, and he'll throw two hundred on top. This will allow us to expand more."

"I'm all about expansion, Nino," Dollar said.

"Plus, the more money means even more of the latest guns," Pistol said, getting excited just thinking about the shit.

"We just have to make sure we move everything we get from this nigga with no excuses. Because we don't want to go to war with this nigga," Nino said.

"Fuck that nigga! We got guns, and he bleeds like

we do," Pistol said, feeling himself a little too much and not knowing what he was going up against with Ramon.

"We got a good thing going, Pistol, and I'm not going to fuck this up." Nino raised his voice a little, which alerted his pit bulls, Donte and Vicious, as they ran into the room from the kitchen over to Nino.

"See, Pistol, you got Nino's dogs up in here thinking it's beef and they're ready to eat yo ass," Dollar said.

The pit bulls were by his side and were ready to attack on his command, even though everything was good. Once the dogs heard his voice, they appeared on command. The doorbell and a knock at the door shifted their attention.

"Any of y'all niqgas expecting anybody?"

"Nah, folk," L-Geez responded.

"I got it," Dollar responded, grabbing his fully-modified Tek-9mm with thirty-two in the clip and one in the chamber. He switched it to auto, which would allow him to spray everything in his way. "Who is it?" he questioned.

"Somebody crashed into the back of that white Hummer and then kept going," a female voice said.

Dollar opened the door and saw a thick brown-skinned shawty standing there looking good.

"Hold on, shawty. Yo, Nino! Baby girl here says someone ran into yo' truck."

"What? Somebody hit my shit?" he yelled as he jumped up and made his way to the front door.

He couldn't see any damage to the back of the truck, so he walked over to the truck to get a closer lock. Nothing. In fact, there was no damage to any part of the truck. What the fuck was this bitch on, or was he becoming paranoid? As these thoughts came to him, it happened.

"This is a stickup, nigga! We here for da paper," a nigga said, accompanied by his homeboy, with both of them pointing their guns at Nino.

He instantly was pissed thinking about how he was going to kill the bitch that said his truck was hit. They brought Nino around to the townhouse in view of Dollar.

Dollar immediately reacted and pulled out his classic .44 Super Blackhawk single-chamber reaction. He cocked the hammer back and fired a powerful and thunderous slug at the bitch that set the shit up. The slug hit her bicep and tore her arm in half, severing it from the bone and flesh. The second slug entered her back and punctured her lung on impact, forcing her to struggle to breathe as she fell to the ground looking over at the niggas that influenced her to help them. Dollar then shifted his weapon on the two niggas that had their guns on Nino.

"Y'all nigga done fucked up!" he snapped.

The sound of gunfire was followed by Dollar's loud voice that alerted Pistol, L-Geez, Donte, and Vicious.

The two pit bulls came out fast and unexpectedly toward the two robbers who had their guns on Nino. With no command, the dogs attacked when they saw that their owner was in distress. Both of the would-be robbers never saw this coming as the pit bulls locked on them. In the same instance, Nino turned as they shifted their attention to the dogs. He pulled out his Glock 40 and dumped rounds on the niggas, silencing them from all the screaming they were doing from the dogs that were locked onto them and shaking them violently.

"Pistol! L-Geez! Grab the money!"

Nino and Dollar dragged the niggas and bitch in between two cars.

"Nino, this bitch really tried to set us up!" Dollar said.

"We're changing the game, so we must change with the game. This spot is dead to us now."

L-Geez and Pistol came out of the house with the money. They were both breathing heavily.

"Yo, we got the paper. Y'all ready to get outta here, or what?" L-Geez said, knowing they could not stay any longer.

"Put the money in my truck. We're flying out today to meet the homie out West. Meet me at the airport within the hour. I'll hit him up to let him know I'm coming that way," he said.

He then left the area, but first he dropped off the dogs at another one of his nice cribs. He also left them water and food, which would last them a few days, even though he knew he would not be gone that long. As he exited the crib and headed to the airport, he took notice of two white males watching him.

The first thought that came to his mind was if the niggas were Feds, but he kept it moving. He wanted to head out West to give Ramon his bread, so the Feds would be the least of his worries. He jumped into his truck and drove past the car with the men in it that looked out of place. Once he arrived at the airport, he put his squad onto what he had seen and thought about them.

"Yo, I think them boys was in front of my spot. So whatever y'all do, be on point and be even more aware of who we bring into our circle," Nino said.

Not realizing the amount of product they moved nor the rate at which they moved it, the Feds were bound to come if there was someone in their circle of whom they were unaware.

~ ~ ~

Five hours later, Nino and his team landed in LA and called up Ramon to let him know that they had landed. Ramon sent a text with the location of one of the many movie theaters that he owned throughout the state.

Nino and his team made their way to the theater. As soon as they got there, he could see Ramon's men outside standing guard. He exited the rental and made his way up to the door with his crew.

"Nino, follow me," the big goon said.

They entered the theater, which boasted a total of eight individual theaters inside. The security took

Nino and his team into a theater, where Ramon sat in the middle by himself watching *King of New York* starring Christopher Walken. Ramon did not even turn around because he knew that it was Nino and his team arriving. He waved them down to where he was sitting. Nino sat at his side while the others sat behind him and Ramon.

Ramon was enjoying the movie as well as the sweet butter popcorn.

"Hermano, you have my money?"

"Here's 1.8, plus I'm trying to get a little more this time with my own money. I would like a better number, too."

Ramon remained watching the movie while still listening to Nino.

"You know what I like about this movie, hermano? He takes what he wants and builds his empire and legacy on the way to the top. I see you come to negotiate in order to build your empire," Ramon said while eating his popcorn and still watching the movie. "Twelve even is your new number. No negotiating so don't ask. With this product I have now, one snort will numb your whole fucking body. You can cut this shit three times and still have grade-A shit."

Nino never checked how raw the cocaine was. All he knew was that people wanted more of it, and his clientele wanted it as fast as he could get it.

"I don't cut the product. I prefer to give it to them as it comes, in order to keep them coming back for more. That means more money for you and me."

"I like the sound of that, hermano," he said, taking a sip of his Coca-Cola on ice. "You have my money with you in the car out front, I assume?" Ramon questioned, finally looking at him.

"Yeah, there's a total of 4.2 and change. Pistol! L-Geez! Go secure the bags."

They both got up and made their way out. Ramon signaled his team to follow.

"It must be nice to have your own theater to watch your favorite movies in."

"I have close to twenty throughout the state, but I like to come to this one for business and peace of mind."

"Maybe one day I will go into the theater business with you on the East Coast, and you could check me out sometime and watch *Scarface* or the *Godfather*."

"I like your drive, hermano. We see money the same, unlike some people who settle for less like cars and jewelry. That shit don't mean anything in the long run."

Ramon's team came back in with L-Geez and

Pistol.

"*Oye viejo, elles tienes chabos,*" the goon said.

Ramon appreciated the sound of money being made and secured while enjoying his favorite movie.

"Nino, I'm going to give you three hundred on top of what you bought so you don't have to make too many trips. But never forget how I feel about my money."

"We feel the same, so you'll always have yours first. I'll call you in a few days," he said, before turning to his team. "We out!"

"Nino, sit down, amigo! The movie is still on; besides, this is the best part."

Nino sat back down along with his crew. At the same time, Ramon's staff brought each of them popcorn, nachos, and mixed drinks to their liking.

"Nino, tonight I want to show you and your crew

my appreciation by inviting you to one of my clubs, so get some new clothes, because we're going to have a good time. Check into a hotel, send me your location, and I'll have cars come pick you all up."

"I'm going to get a suite at the Crown Plaza, after I take my crew shopping for tonight's fun."

Nino's team couldn't believe how this nigga Ramon had his own theater. To them, that was next-level getting-money.

CHAPTER 7

THE NIGHT CAME quickly, and the city of Los Angeles came alive with the nightlife. Models, celebrities, athletes, and ballas all came out to enjoy their wealth. Among these elites, Nino and his team pulled up to the club in the S600 Mercedes Benz limo that Ramon sent to pick them up. They all stepped out wearing the latest fashions from YSL to Tom Ford, watches from Movado to Breitling, and diamonds on their necks, wrists, and studded earrings. They definitely looked the part of new-money millionaires. Ramon also came through in the custom-painted black pearl Rolls Royce Phantom, along with his goons rolling behind him in three separate black Range Rover Sports.

Nino and his team stood by outside of the limo waiting on Ramon to exit like a boss, with his team exiting their trucks first. Then he stepped out looking dapper in a gray silk Armani suit tailored to perfection.

"Welcome to Club Mint, gentlemen. Tonight, is on me—drinks, food, fun, and women," Ramon said as he led the way into the club.

Nino's crew was instantly impressed by the layout of the club with $100s, $50s, and $20s in the illuminated mint-green floor, walls, bar countertops, and tables throughout the club.

"Ramon, you used real bills for all of this?"

"Of course, after you have so much money, it all becomes paper. So I took $1 million in cash and had the contractors laminate it into the floors as well as into the walls and around the bars. The VIP section has all $100s with mint-green lighting to give the club a feel of opulence to inspire all of my customers. Everyone that comes in here can afford to be around this money, and it doesn't faze them because they have wealth or are working their way up to it. Besides, if anyone did try to steal it, my cameras or security would catch them. They wouldn't even have a chance to buy a drink with the money."

"This is the best-looking club I've ever been to," Pistol said.

"I know. I say that every time I come in here," Ramon responded, being confident and humorous at the same time.

Ramon gestured to his staff as his sexy bartenders walked over to serve him and his guests. All the women that worked there looked like they had just stepped out of a photo shoot. They all had to look the part for the celebrity clientele.

"Yo, Nino, look over there! There's the two model shawties, Gigi and Bella Hadid," Dollar said, a little star struck.

"They're regulars here, amongst others who come to enjoy themselves and their wealth!" Ramon said.

Nino gestured to his homie to calm down and not get so excited, because they, too, were in a different league minus the fame. So now they had to start embracing the new environment that Ramon had them in, because this was everyday life out in LA.

The night went on as they partied Ramon's way with women, food, and drinks. They were living the good life, meeting and greeting Ramon's famous friends: players from the Lakers and 49ers, models, movie stars, and more. Nino and his team embraced this new life, each appreciating seeing all of the famous people, especially the model sisters. They took selfies on their phones, which was certainly something these niggas did not do in the hood because of the life they were living. Lebron even came through and made an appearance with his entourage.

After the night came to an end, they all made their way back outside and waited for their cars to be brought to them. Ramon's men stood around securing him as he waited on his guests to leave first. At the same time, he made sure the celebrities and social elites made it out safely.

When two white girls started fighting because they were drunk, Ramon looked on at his security and nodded to them to break it up. As they went to part the two women, an Italian Mafioso-looking muthafucka came out of nowhere.

"Don't fucking touch my lady, or we're going to have some problems here!" the Italian man threatened.

Ramon looked on at his men and prepared to say something to the Italian punk, after feeling disrespected by him. However, Dollar, Pistol, and L-Geez pulled out their weapons and aimed them in the guy's face as well as the faces of the two guys he was with who stepped up like they wanted beef. The Italian man snapped with arrogance.

"Do you know who the fuck I am? I'm Joey Catillino, a fucking made man! I'll have all you mulis and spics dealt with!"

Ramon didn't take too much to this small-time Mafioso. He displayed his distaste calmly and responded completely in control of the situation.

"Personally, cabron, I don't give a fuck who you are or what Mafia family you represent, because I'll wipe all of you *goombatas* out. What I do have a problem with is you disrespecting my guests, my club, and me."

"What? Are you fucking kidding me? You got a

little money so you think you're somebody? I know you better tell those niggas to get their guns out of my face!"

Pistol snapped and took his gun and cracked the mobster over the head and across the face. The man staggered backward in a daze while at the same time his face stung from the brute force. Joey fell back and reached for his face after feeling the warm blood coming down the side from the cut over his eye. He tried to reach for the gun on his waist until Pistol stopped him in his tracks, jamming his gun in his face with his finger on the trigger.

"Who the fuck you calling a nigga, you bitch-ass muthafucka!" Pistol yelled.

"You're a dead nigga for pistol whipping me! You kill me, and you'll be floating in the ocean as shark food!"

Pistol was tired of holding back. He normally would have killed this piece of shit for his disrespect. Instead, he placed the gun to his stomach and was going to fire off a round while looking into Joey's eyes, so he knew he was not the only killa.

"No!" Ramon yelled out, stopping Pistol from killing the scum. "My men will deal with him, his crew, and these trouble-making bitches," Ramon said.

His men would take care of Joey and his crew as they led them away from the club. Ramon then leaned over to his security closest to him.

"Make sure they're never found."

Ramon's security already knew what that meant. He wanted them all dead, even the drunk chicks who were fighting. They would never be found. Ramon knew a crematorium that knew how to burn bodies to make them completely disappear.

"Nino, I like the way your crew moves. The young one is also a good asset for you. I can see we will have a bright future with your loyalty and crew. Call me in a few days to confirm your shipment."

"I enjoyed myself tonight, minus this knucklehead and his friends. The women out here are special and exotic looking. I can't wait to come back this way," Nino said as he walked toward the limo with his team.

They all headed back to the hotel to rest for the night before they flew back East the next morning.

CHAPTER 8

AT NOON THE next day in LA, Tommy Guns made a call to Ramon as planned to make him aware that he was in the city.

"*Que pasa, mi amigo?*"

"What's good, Ramon? I'm calling to let you know I'm here. Where do you want me to meet you at?"

Ramon looked at his watch and checked the time.

"It's lunchtime now, so meet me at my restaurant in town."

"Say no more. I'm on my way."

Tommy was fully aware of the type of person he was dealing with in Ramon, so he prepared Tre and his team on the way over so they knew what they were getting into and how to approach him. Because at the end of the day, Ramon would bleed just like they did.

It didn't take long before they arrived at the restaurant. Tre and Raven walked in as a couple and ordered food and drinks. Trigger entered a few minutes behind and made his way up to the counter to order food as well. Jay was across the street with strict orders not to let anyone leave if he heard shit pop off. Tommy had secured guns for the entire crew through some people he met in the area before he headed back East and linked up with everyone. Tommy came in with no gun because he knew Ramon would have him checked, because it was what he did.

A waitress walked over to Tommy, who was sitting at his table, and whispered to him, "Ramon wants you to come into the back office."

Tommy was surprised and did not think Ramon would be there before him.

Ramon always liked to make an entrance; however, he was there before Tommy. This was another red flag that stood out as Tommy stood up to make his way to the back office. This sudden change also made Tommy Guns start to think of ways to prevail from what he was thinking may take place. He knew if he did not go to the back office that shit would hit the fan, so he made eye contact with the waitress knowing he was probably being watched—and he was.

"Thank you, I'm on my way now, beautiful," he said, making her smile briefly because she worked for Ramon outside of her waitress job.

Tre and Raven were also shocked by the sudden change of events. This was not how Tommy laid it out to them on the way over.

"Oh shit, mami! He changed up on us," Tre said.

"We still have to hold him down, papi! No matter what," Raven said, looking into Tre's eyes and rubbing his hand across the table. "I love you, papi, 'til the wheels fall off," she said, knowing that something was about to go down.

"'Til the wheels fall off, mami," he responded before focusing on what was to come.

On his way back to the office, Tommy swiped a knife off the countertop in the kitchen and cuffed it into his sleeve. The waitress knocked on the door, and one of Ramon's security goons answered the door. She gave a brief smile before walking away, since Tommy's presence spoke for itself. Once inside the office, he took notice of the silenced 9mm sitting on Ramon's desk. He figured if Ramon went for the gun, he would stab the big bodyguard and use him as a shield before he fled the office.

Ramon stared at Tommy as the door shut behind him. He seemed to have a distant look in his eyes. It was not the welcoming look that he usually had when he met with Tommy Guns.

"The people I'm associated with, who make everything that I do possible, felt that I needed to get rid of you before you become a problem that would affect what we have going on. I was going to do just that until I had a change of heart and mind, because we have a mutual respect for the lives we live. However, mi amigo, you brought your crew out here as if you wanted to counter my attack. You have those cabrons across the street and those puntas in my restaurant."

Ramon was pissed off and ready to take care of business, cleaning up Tommy Guns and his crew. As he was speaking, there was a knock at the door. When the goon opened the door, the chef stood there looking as if he needed to get permission to make something for Ramon. Suddenly, Raven popped out from behind the chef with her twin nickel-plated .32 automatics with black pearl grips and fired off headshots to each of the goons in the room with swift precision. She got the attention and respect she wanted before shifting her guns at Ramon's face.

"Don't even think about reaching for that gun, punta, or your brains will be all over the back of that expensive leather chair you're sitting in!" Raven warned, eyeing him down and practically daring him to move just to prove her point.

Tre entered right behind Raven to secure anything that moved. Tommy stepped closer to the desk and eyed down Ramon. Two stone-cold killers eyed each other down.

"Ramon, we could have taken this country by storm with your connections and my means to always get it done. But you chose how this ends, you stupid muthafucka!" Tommy Guns snapped, taking the silenced 9mm from the desk and leaving Raven to finish the job.

"I fucking saved your life, and this is how you repay me?" Ramon pleaded, finally being powerless and facing down the barrels of Raven's guns.

"We make choices, and you obviously made the wrong one. Raven, don't let him say another word!" Tommy Guns said.

Raven fired off two back-to-back rounds which cracked his skull on impact and ejected his brains out the other side, spraying the leather chair and wall with warm flesh and chunks of his skull.

"OG, we can't leave any witnesses up in here," Tre said as they prepared to leave the office.

Ramon's men in the office were already dead. He had a few more outside of the restaurant, and those working inside might also be on his team. So after they exited the office, they laid out everyone including the chef, waitresses, and other employees who could identify him.

Trigger and the rest of the young bucks heard gunfire inside as did Ramon's men, so they started shooting it out with them, too. Tommy Guns, Raven, and Tre all came out firing on them and taking all of them out one by one.

They could not waste any time, so they rushed back to the airport and headed back East far away from the chaotic shit. Tommy was now feeling good about his life of freedom and being back with his little homie. Now he needed to link back up with Ra Ra.

"Tre, that baby girl you got is all about that life how she put work in."

Raven smiled and enjoyed the compliment from an

OG.

"Good looking, little ma, you held me down and came through on a surprise by laying down them goons."

"Anytime, papi! My man says you good peoples, so I hold you down."

Tommy put his head back as the plane climbed into the skies to take them back East. When his eyes closed, he thought about what had taken place back at the restaurant.

"Would you like anything to drink, sir?" the flight attendant asked Tommy as he opened his eyes to see a beautiful sista glowing in her uniform with her radiant smile. He glanced at her name tag. "A double shot of Hennessy would be fine, Lena," he said to her.

Her eyes showed surprise that he knew her name, until she realized he had read her name tag.

"That's unique, and it almost caught me off guard. But I appreciate that you took the time to look at my name tag," she said, making small talk while giving him his double shot of Hennessy and moving on to the next person.

Tommy downed the Hennessy and placed the plastic cup down. He enjoyed the warmth of the cognac flowing down his throat and into his belly. Then he noticed out of the corner of his eye that someone was watching him. Who? He turned toward the man sitting in the other aisle; however, the man turned around quickly as if he did not want any confrontation. Tommy then turned back to his crew and saw Raven laying her head on Tre's shoulder with her eyes closed. Trigger and the young bucks were all eating their meals that were just served to them. He then noticed the man staring at him again.

"What are you looking at?" Tommy asked with a dark stare.

The businessman sitting across the aisle was on a laptop, but he was well groomed, clean-shaven, and wearing a nice navy-blue suit. He had a dark stare with a serious look as he addressed Tommy Guns and his question.

"Calm down, Mr. Mitchell, or should I say, Mr. Anderson?"

When Tommy heard himself being addressed in that manner by the man wearing a suit, the Feds came to mind. At the same time, he thought about who else would know who he really was.

"Who the fuck are you?" he asked, getting the attention of the flight attendant passing out food.

"Is everything all right with you two?" Lena asked.

"Just fine, Lena. Questions of curiosity that we all

have," the white man said with a fake smile.

She walked away, and then he addressed Tommy as he turned his laptop around so Tommy could see.

"Look here, Mr. Anderson."

Tommy could not believe what he was seeing. It was footage of what just had taken place inside and outside of Ramon's restaurant. The massacre was all caught on tape, and everyone's faces could be seen clearly.

"You see, Mr. Anderson, your presence has long expired. Ramon should have never kept you around, but he did, and as we see, you were a liability then and even more now since he's dead. And with his death, you, Mr. Anderson, inherit his $300 million debt owed to my associates."

"So you think I'm going to pay his debt? You muthafucka is crazy!"

"We don't think you'll pay his debt. We know that from the moment you took his life that you decided to get us our money. Now you do have a choice that most individuals never opt to choose: pay in blood with your life. However, that will come after you see the demise of everyone you love. We know what's important to you—Candy and the son you two have, and the two boys who live with your mother. We have our best interest in this secured, and from every angle you think of, we've thought of it," the man said, never flinching or fearing anything about Tommy Guns because he knew that he could easily erase him and his family.

"Don't fuck with my kids or my family, or I'll choke yo' bitch ass out right now!" Tommy said.

Tommy reacted quickly and jumped up. He caught the man off guard and began to choke him; however, even under this condition with Tommy choking him, he managed to stay calm.

"Mr. Anderson, your family will die if you don't stop choking me long enough so I can send this e-mail out to my associates."

Tommy released his grip and allowed the man to gasp for air.

"Now that we have your anger in check, I'll do my behalf at keeping your family alive and allow my associates to know that we have your full cooperation," he said, running his fingers across the keyboard of the laptop before looking back up at Tommy. "That's all for now. One more thing, Mr. Anderson: everything back at Ramon's place is already cleaned up and disposed of like it never happened. It will open under a new name and management, and you will own and operate his businesses for shipment purposes. You'll embrace it all. This selling drugs thing is your profession. You'll be contacted with more information soon."

Tommy wanted to choke the muthafucka again, but he did not want to risk losing his family or Candy. Now he was forced to come out of the low-key lifestyle he was gearing up for to take care of these people, whoever they were, and have a $300 million distribution that Ramon needed to pay. This new life of having to pay a debt like that was far from what Tommy had in mind for his future.

CHAPTER 9

THE NEXT DAY in Atlanta, Tommy and Candy were watching TV as she affectionately cuddled up next to him. Their son played with his toys and crawled on the floor not far from the couch where they sat. Tommy really appreciated this second chance at life being with Candy. However, after meeting the man on the plane and having to take over Ramon's duties, he was not feeling that at all, but it had to be done. This was all until he reached the amount they wanted from him.

"Tommy, I forgot to tell you your mom called saying how much she loves you and appreciates the money," Candy said, lifting her head off of his body.

The doorbell rang twice, which immediately got their attention.

"I got it," he said, taking his .45 Desert Eagle with

him to answer the door since he had no idea who it could be.

When he got to the door, he saw that it was the mailman.

"Good morning, sir, I have a package for Michael Mitchell."

"Who is it from?" he asked.

"Uh, Mr. Ramon Perez."

Tommy signed for the next-day-air package, knowing that it was from the man with whom he'd spoken on the plane.

"Candy, stay in here while I look at this stuff," he said.

He made his way into the dining room to open the package, which contained a cell phone and a typed letter that read:

ENCLOSED YOU'LL FIND A CELL PHONE CONTAIN-

ING ALL OF RAMON'S CLIENTELE, THE KEYS TO HIS BUSINESSES, AND THE ADDRESS TO THE WAREHOUSE WITH THE FIFTEEN TONS. WE SECURED $50 MILLION OF HIS DEBT THROUGH HIS OFF-SHORE ACCOUNTS, MINUS THE $10 MILLION FOR HIS MANSION, SO WE'RE NOW AT $240 MIL. REMEMBER, WE'RE WATCHING AT ALL TIMES.

Tommy looked at the addresses of the warehouse and businesses. He then turned on the cell phone, scrolled through the numbers, and saw his clientele of boss niggas and bitches picking up heavy shit. He tore off the top of the letter with the addresses and then put the paper and keys into his pocket.

"Is everything okay?"

"Yeah, we good!" he said before giving Candy a hug and a kiss on her cheek.

She figured whatever it was that was bothering him would come out sooner or later.

~ ~ ~

Meanwhile in North Carolina, Nino and his team were preparing to meet with a Puerto Rican man they met in New York who would be copping heavy. L-Geez and Dollar met him in their travels.

Nino arranged the meeting outside of the hood at a five-star restaurant called Emari's, which was known for its world-renowned guest chefs each month. Nino felt this would be a good look to impress the new customers with the sumptuous side of business. Nino also wanted to see who it was who wanted two hundred bricks all in one shot. It allowed him to get a feel for who he was allowing into the circle.

Nino, Dollar, L-Geez, and Pistol all sat outside of the restaurant waiting on their guest to arrive. Within minutes, a deep, dark red Porsche Cayenne turbo truck came through with chrome 24s. L-Geez and Dollar got out of their whips and made their way over to their new client. Nino and Pistol stayed in their cars and checked out the approach of this man.

"Yo, Juan, what's up, folk?" L-Geez asked.

"I'm focused on this new BI y'all talking about."

"Whoa, who dat in the whip?" Dollar asked when he saw that he did not come alone.

Juan turned around to the truck and nodded to his associate, so she could get out of the car while he explained who she was.

"This is my ride-or-die chick, Ri Ri. She's about me."

Ri Ri exited the truck looking real sexy with her light Latina skin and gray-colored cat eyes. She further stood out with her long, silky black hair braided back and hanging over a baby-blue fur coat, white Prada shirt, blue jeans hugging her thick thighs and ass, and high heels by Cavalli, which just added to her five-foot-six height. She was a real sexy ride-or-die chick to match her fly Spanish papi, Juan, who came wearing a chinchilla quarter-length, a diamond chain with the Virgin Mary, and a diamond watch by Jacobs.

Once they saw that she was official, they took Juan and Ri Ri over to Nino in his truck. He saw them coming, so he stepped out of his truck. He did not say a word to Juan or his chick; he just walked into the restaurant and over to the reserved table they had. Then they all ordered food and drinks.

Once the drinks were served, the introductions also came. Nino wanted the silence of not speaking to them to see if he could make them feel uncomfortable since they grabbed a lot of work. He wanted to make sure they were who they said they were.

"So, Juan, I'm told you're looking for a heavy two-piece. My question is where is the connect you used to deal with? Why the sudden change?"

Juan took a bite of his buttered lobster and enjoyed its freshness as he chased it with a glass of red wine before answering Nino's question.

"This lobster is superb, and the wine takes it to another level," he said while wiping his mouth. "Now as for my connect, King Jose of New York was killed over a year ago. Since then I've been dealing in small quantities because that's all they could handle. I can't contain my limits because they can't afford to keep up with supply. Now that explains the why. Now as far as when I need the product, now would make sense because the streets are calling."

Nino realized that if he got these bricks off to this cat, he would be back on track to moving them as fast as he did the last shipment. This would be a good look for him in Ramon's eyes. But little did he know that

Ramon no longer existed.

"I can get it to you in a day or so, unless you want to pick it up yourself?"

"I'll do whatever is faster. Now let's talk numbers."

Nino looked over at Dollar and L-Geez to see if they already had given him a number. He did not want to cut them out of their share.

"What did my little homies tell you the price was?"

"Nino, we didn't. We wanted to wait to see what you said, since he's grabbing heavy," Dollar said.

"Well then, sixteen per block," Nino shot out there.

Juan looked at Nino as he was drinking his wine and processing the number thrown his way at the same time.

"Hmmm, sixteen is too high, amigo, for the quantity I'm buying. That number leaves me no room to play."

"You'll triple your money fucking with this product."

Juan turned to Ri Ri to ask her what she thought, since she was really the boss. She gave him a sexy smile as her way of saying yes. He then focused back on Nino.

"I'm in! We have a deal, amigo."

"I'll have the homies contact you when everything is ready. Let's make a toast to good business and a promising future," Nino said, raising his glass.

Ri Ri looked over at Nino with bedroom eyes as if she wanted to fuck him. Maybe she saw dollar signs in how he ran his business. Nino also caught the look, but being business-minded, he did not even entertain the idea. With this type of money on the line, it would not be good for business.

CHAPTER 10

TWO DAYS LATER, just like clockwork, Nino's shipment came through, so he called Ramon, only to get an answer from a voice on the other end of the phone which he did not recognize.

"Yo, who's this answering Ramon's phone?"

"This is Mike. All business will now be conducted through me. Ramon has been retired from his position of power. I'm running the show now."

"It is what it is, Mike. I'm calling to let y'all know everything is official."

"Say no more! You know what you have to do when you're done."

After the call, Nino reached out to Juan and made arrangements for him to get his work. Then he called up L-Geez and Dollar to let them know that he was going to meet up at the Waffle House.

Nino let Pistol go back to Miami to secure things down there; besides, he wanted to go see his girl, Diamond.

Juan was at the hotel not too far from the Waffle House when Nino called. Nino wanted to handle this shit personally before securing other business. Within ten minutes, Juan came pulled up beside Nino's H2 Hummer. He and Ri Ri stepped out still looking like money with their New York swagga on ten wearing the latest fashions. He popped the rear door on the Porsche truck while Nino did the same and opened up the back of his Hummer.

"Where's my money, Juan?" Nino asked, getting straight to it.

"*Tranquillo, amigo!* It's all business here. I told you the streets are calling and waiting for me to get back up top," Juan said as he reached in the back and grabbed the bag of money.

Nino took it back to the Hummer and then unzipped the bag and checked to see if the money was all there. From a visual glance, it looked to be all there. Nino then grabbed the bags out of his truck with the bricks before he headed back to the Porsche truck.

"That's what I'm talking about!" Juan said, excited.

As if Juan's statement was a cue, the Federal agents came fast from every angle and swooped in on Nino. He could see the cars closing in on him, so he reached for his gun, not knowing that Juan and Ri Ri were on their side until she pulled out her gun and placed it against the back of his head.

"Don't even think about it, punta, or your brains will be all over the Hummer. You're under arrest, and it's too bad we're on the opposite side, because I really think you're fine."

The swarm of Feds took Nino over to a car and placed him in the back seat. Agent Juan Rodriguez was standing in front of his truck talking to the other agents about the bust. L-Geez saw the entire scene and started his truck, mashing the gas and racing toward Juan and the other agents. They did not even see him coming until it was too late. He crushed them in between his truck and Juan's Porsche, instantly squeezing the life from them.

Dollar pulled out his MAC-10 fully automatic with extended clips. He sprayed slugs at the Federal agents, catching them off guard as their attention shifted toward L-Geez crashing into the other agents.

L-Geez jumped out of his truck as the agents started firing on him. L-Geez used his AR-15 to spray on them as he took them out by surprise, because they did not expect any confrontation. L-Geez came around to the back of the truck behind Ri Ri.

"You pretty bitch, you set my nigga up!"

She tried to turn around knowing she could not die today; however, her speed was not fast enough. He sprayed her with a burst of rounds which thrust her body back as slugs crashed into her body and face, sucking the life from her flesh before she even hit the ground.

L-Geez grabbed the cocaine and put it back into the Hummer before he jumped behind the wheel. He again mashed the gas and raced toward the agents that were shooting at Dollar. He ran over a few more in between spraying them with his AR-15.

As the bullets continued spraying out of the window and forcing the agents to take cover, L-Geez plowed through the agents' cars and raced out of the Waffle House parking lot.

The Federal agents called for backup, and at the same time made them aware of the shooter in the Hummer.

Dollar was unable to get into his truck to escape as agents continued firing on him, but he kept them back with bursts of fire from his weapon. He then took advantage of the situation by jumping into his G55 and slamming his foot down on the gas, which forced the modified V10 engine to thrust the Benz forward and blast through the cars by the entrance that tried to block him in. The clashing of the metal on metal sounded just as loud as the continuous gunfire.

Dollar caught slugs in his leg, arm, back, and shoulder as he plowed through all of the agents. Those able to jump into their cars chased behind him with their adrenaline fired up and rushing through their bodies. All of their training led to this very moment.

Nino was still in the back seat of the Feds' car looking on at his little homies banging out with the Feds.

"Muthafuckas! I can't believe this shit!" Dollar said, feeling the burning from the slugs lodged in him. He switched clips in his gun for fear of getting caught, because he was not going to jail without putting up a fight. He did not even want his old head, Nino, to get locked up, but this shit went sideways.

Dollar was trying to make it back to his hood in the projects because he would lose the Feds on his trail; besides, the cops that knew about his projects did not rush to go through there unassisted. The truck was going close to one hundred miles per hour down a forty-five mile per hour street. He thought he was getting distance between him and the Feds until he saw the Greensboro police in front of him blocking the road ahead.

"Damn! Fuck it! Y'all niggas want to block the road? Fuck all of y'all!" he snapped, slamming his foot to the floor and not even caring what happened next.

He knew and could feel it in his body that the end was near. The Greensboro police were not prepared for what was about to happen next. Dollar stuck his gun out of the window and fired off as his truck was approaching now at a speed over one hundred miles per hour. Each of the slugs crashed into officers as well as the cars in front of the bullets that were being fired. Dollar came up quick on the roadblock, breaking through it, with the metal clashing and sounding loud. The officers that did not move fast enough were hit by bullets and other cars as he blasted through their roadblock. They did not expect for him to drive into their roadblock, just as he did not expect to have his $100,000 plus truck flip on him in the process of breaking through the roadblock. His truck slid close to one hundred yards before coming to a halt.

Battered and bruised, Dollar still tried to escape by firing off rounds from his position of being sideways. The officers and Federal agents all closed in on him while unleashing a barrage of bullets on the G55 Benz truck. They soon realized they needed to stabilize the threat of Dollar firing on them. Over one hundred rounds were fired from the agents and officers before they found their target, killing Dollar over and over. They secured the scene once they saw that he was no longer moving. He went out just like a true gangsta, taking as many of them out as he could before they got to him.

On the other side of the city, L-Geez made it to their other stash house to secure the rest of the cocaine, knowing it was no longer safe there. He called up one of his shawties that was all about her business when he called. She came quick, and he put her onto what was going on.

"Aw, shawty, I'ma give ya ten bands. Take this Hummer and get it chopped up over at the Spanish nigga's spot. I'ma use yo' whip for a few days, ya hear me? I'll get back to you then."

"Take care of yo' self, L-Geez," she said, kissing him before he jumped into her black Honda Accord with tinted windows, which was the perfect car to be low key in.

He called up Pistol as soon as he pulled off, to put him onto what had happened. His adrenaline was still revved up.

"Pistol, this shit just got crazy up here. The Feds ran down on the big homie."

"How the fuck did that happen?"

"Them folks from New York are with the Feds, man. They're the fucking FBI. I didn't see that shit coming. Me and Dollar were trying to break him free, but it didn't work out. I got away, but I don't know if Dollar did."

"You have to leave the state, folk. Come down here with me in Miami. We'll secure shit from here," Pistol said while still trying to remain focused.

"I'll call ya when I get in the city," L-Geez said as he got onto the highway and headed for Florida, ready to start over and get as far away as he could from the Carolinas right then.

CHAPTER 11

OVER AT THE Greensboro FBI office, Nino was being detained and questioned on the whereabouts of L-Geez. He was his connect that supplied him with all of the cocaine, because they knew this was bigger than him, and it could lead to joint US and Mexico task forces taking down the cartel.

"We want to know where the guy in the truck went. We know that you know!" the agent yelled.

"If I knew, you still wouldn't know, because it's not my job to tell you who he is!" Nino snapped.

"Listen here, wise ass! You're going to get hit with the RICO Act, and you'll never see the light of day. If that isn't enough to get your attention, you'll also be charged with the murders of those agents back there. Federal death row is where you'll go! Oh, your boy Dollar is dead, in case you thought he got away! He was gunned down just like the animal he was!" the agent informed.

Nino put his head back and thought about his little homie, but the agent yelled out and cut into his thoughts. "You're going down for this! Death row, here he comes!"

Nino locked eyes with the agent and stared him down. He personally wanted to kill him on the spot. Another agent entered the room with a serious look on his face. He wanted to get to the core of the cocaine trail.

"Mr. Jones, I'm Agent Miles from the Harrisburg Bureau. I was sent down here on strict orders from the director of the FBI. We knew these guys were onto you. We needed to wait for the right time to step in," he began as Nino looked on and wondered where this was going. "Rakman Hussein is the reason I'm here. You and Mr. Hussein became good friends while in prison, and we have you two on video passing mail back and forth. We didn't piece it all together until he managed to escape, and then you were released not long after. You got caught with twenty kilos. There is no other way out of Dauphin County Prison unless you had help, and we believe you did," Agent Miles said, precisely connecting all the dots.

Nino was shocked that the Fed nigga knew all of this. He figured he and Rakman had a tight movement together. Nino thought about the other agent's words about being on death row or spending his life in jail. He was not about that life.

"What do you want to know about Rakman?"

"I want to know who he was contacting and who helped him escape?"

Nino gave him the entire breakdown of the process, the letters that were written in Arabic, and the address with the names and more.

"What's the address and phone number, Mr. Jones?" Agent Miles asked.

"I didn't memorize it, but my brother kept it just in case I needed it."

"It looks like you need it now, Mr. Jones," Agent Miles said. "Gentlemen, he said his brother has the info, so get on it," Miles added, upon seeing the agents still standing around as if they were not paying attention.

Another agent walked into the room with a phone and handed it to Nino.

"I gave y'all the address and phone number, so let me go now," Nino said.

"You're going to sit here until we confirm that information," Agent Miles responded.

Within a few hours all the information Nino had given them came through, which led back to the senator and governor of California. Each denied the allegations against them; however, neither of them was able to explain how Rakman had their phone numbers and addresses.

Agent Miles ordered the release of Nino, so once again he was a free man because of a corrupt government wanting to appease itself. Similar to the Gotti situation when his number-two guy sold him out after killing nineteen men, the government let Nino go in exchange for all the information he knew on the boss.

Meanwhile, Agent Miles sent the new information to CNN and the local news in Harrisburg to make sure that the truth would be exposed.

As the news spread nationwide, the FBI was forced to bring the California governor and senator in on charges for aiding in an escape, amongst other things. As they were being led into the FBI Headquarters in California, multiple news outlets rushed them for questions.

"I'm innocent! I don't know what's going on here!" the senator yelled out in fear of his world collapsing around him.

The governor broke down crying and pleading to the media: "We didn't do anything! They must be mistaking us for someone else!"

As they were in front of the cameras making their empty pleas, the CIA director, along with other elite agencies, was now watching all of this unfold.

"Gentlemen, we definitely have a problem that needs to be resolved before it gets out of hand," the director said over the conference call.

"I'll have it all secured within seventy-two hours," the other director said, sounding pissed off.

Down in Juarez, Mexico, Hector Guzman was also watching the chaos unfold in America. These two men once came to his home, and now they were both in a bad position. He hoped they would not bring any heat back onto him. Hector reached out to his associates at the agencies to see if they, too, were aware of what was going on.

Rakman was in Saudi Arabia, so when he was

notified of what was happening, he made arrangements to go to Mexico to meet up with the other associates to discuss and secure the problem.

Meanwhile, over in Washington, DC, Director Davenport received a call from Homeland Security director Tony Ridge.

"Mike, what's going on? Who leaked this info about those men in California? You know we're supposed to find out more first."

"Sir, I don't know what took place, but it cannot be taken back now that it's out there. We just have to let it all play out and allow these men to expose themselves."

"Mike, you're responsible for resolving this. I just received a call from the president. He's not too happy about what's going on, because now he has to address the nation on these accusations made against men in our government."

"I'll take care of this, sir; however, these men in

California put themselves in that position."

"You have forty-eight hours to come up with something other than that. The president needs more," he said before hanging up and leaving Director Davenport to think about what was going on and what still needed to be done.

CHAPTER 12

AT 1:03 A.M., Tommy Guns's cell phone sounded off and woke him. He grabbed the phone but did not recognize the number that was calling.

"Who the fuck is this waking me up?"

"Get up, Mr. Anderson," a calm yet powerful voice ordered.

"I'm up! What's going on?" he asked, now recognizing the voice of the man who he had met on the plane.

"Your business associate, Mr. Jones, a.k.a. Nino, was arrested by the Feds earlier today. He was in posession of two hundred kilos, but somehow that wasn't in the report. It got back to our agency that he had been released due to his cooperation of giving information on Rakman Hussein, which has now caused a ripple effect in our government."

At the sound of Rakman's name, Tommy fully woke up. He thought back to how his life had gotten turned upside down because of the muthafucka who tried to kill him multiple times.

"So what is it you need me to do?"

"Mr. Jones's employment with us is no longer needed. I'll text you his info. We need this done now, so you'll need to fly to North Carolina. And $10 million will be deducted for your services." The voice hung up, leaving Tommy Guns to think about how he would have killed Nino for less than $10 million.

But since it was helping him clear up his debt, Nino was as good as dead.

Tommy kissed Candy's soft lips and let her know business was calling.

"I'll be back by lunch."

"I'll have your lunch and dessert waiting on you right here, so don't miss out," she said, being sexual and funny at the same time.

Tommy took a flight to North Carolina and made his way to Greensboro to the house where Nino lived. The agency provided him with all that he needed, including having someone at the airport give him twin silenced stealth-black 9mms, which he removed upon entering Nino's home, undetected thus far.

As Tommy made his way through the house, he prepared to head upstairs, but Nino's two pit bulls sensed danger and quickly came out of the basement. Their barking and charging toward him drew his immediate attention, and then he saw their eyes illuminated in the darkness.

Instinctively, Tommy Guns took off upstairs until he reached the top of the steps. He quickly turned around as the two pit bulls turned the corner and began to run up the steps, until they were each greeted with silenced slugs to their open mouths. Both dogs were killed instantly as they tumbled back down. After killing the dogs, he cleared each room. No one was at the house, so he needed to head to the second location now. Tommy hoped the nigga did not have pit bulls at the other crib.

It did not take long before he made his way to the second house, where he found no dogs. He closed in while walking down the hall, but he stopped in his tracks when he saw a brown-skinned chick come out of a room with no clothes on, on her way to the hall bathroom. Her eyes lit up and her body froze like a deer in the headlights when she saw a man in black standing there with two silenced 9mms pointed in her face. She looked back into the room from which she had just walked, signifying to Tommy that Nino was probably inside. She then opened her mouth preparing to scream, until Tommy squeezed each of the silenced 9mms once and sent two rounds racing through the air. As she sucked in a mouth of air to scream, she halted as each slug slammed into her mouth and face, twisting her body around and dropping her. At the same time, brains and chunks of her skull flew out the other end and sprayed the wall behind her.

The sound of her body thumping to the floor alerted Nino, which made him look toward the door. He saw her body fall to the ground in the hall. His heart started racing not knowing what to think was happening, but he reached for his gun ready to get it popping.

He rushed over to the doorway with his Glock 40mm in hand. He stepped out of the room with his gun out in front of him. He was ready for whatever, but he did not see Tommy in the shadows hidden in his all-black attire. What he did see were the flashes of the silenced 9mms as the slugs slammed into his body and forced him back into the bedroom.

"Son of a bitch!" Nino let out, upon feeling the burning of his flesh from the slugs that had slammed into his chest, wounding him badly. "This nigga must not know who he's fucking with!"

Nino let out the adrenaline flowing that was keeping him alert. But at the same time, he wanted to kill the nigga that shot him. Tommy moved in quick down the hall and closed in on the bedroom. Nino pulled himself away from the door and backed himself into the corner by the bed. Tommy stuck his head around into the room. Nino spotted him, so he fired off rounds that slammed into the door frame, tearing chunks out of it. Tommy pulled back just in time, only to return fire after Nino was done. His slugs found their target, and he knew it when he heard Nino's groans from the impact of the hot slugs burning his flesh.

"I'ma kill yo bitch ass, nigga!" Nino let out in pain, still unaware of who was shooting at him.

Suddenly, he unloaded the Glock 40mm into the wall where Tommy was standing. Debris flew everywhere as the slugs crashed into the wall and tore out chunks of drywall. Tommy heard the gun click, which signified that it was empty. In a swift motion, he popped into the room with guns out in front of him while aiming at the wounded Nino.

"What you know about Rakman Hussein?"

"You coming at me about this muthafucka?"

"I owe him. I just want to know where he is. You

tell me, and I walk out and let you live."

Nino now realized the money and gift of freedom that he had gotten from Rakman had become a curse, especially since he did not listen to him and not sell drugs.

Nino gave Tommy the same information he gave the Feds, with the addition of where his wife lived in Texas close to the Mexican border. Tommy memorized the address. He definitely wanted to kill Rakman for all of the attempts he had made on his life.

"You're a rat, Nino! You have to die!" Tommy Guns said, firing two silenced rounds into his face and killing him.

Tommy turned and exited, and then made his way back to Atlanta, thinking about how he was going to track down Rakman and personally kill him.

CHAPTER 13

AGENT MILES PULLED up to his home in Harrisburg at 5:00 p.m. He was on his cell phone speaking with Director Davenport. He was making Agent Miles aware of all the heat he was getting from his superiors regarding the information being leaked to the media outlets.

"Sir, I believe these men needed to be exposed for their role in the escape of Rakman Hussein. Agents like myself have been compromised in their actions."

"Agent Miles, I'm behind you, to an extent, as long as I don't lose my job or life behind this."

They talked a few more minutes before the call ended. Mike called up Tony Ridge and briefed him on what was going on from his end. Tony now had to relay this information to the president. As he dialed the number on his cell phone, the office phone started ringing, which got his attention, so he paused to take the call.

"Tony Ridge with Homeland Security, how can I help you?"

"Tony, I guess you're going to support the accusation you just received from Jason Miles. I suggest you don't follow through or your career and life will be at stake."

"Who the hell do you think you are, calling and talking to me like that?"

The phone hung up, which pissed Tony off even more. He needed to relay this info to the president. Tony made a call to his long-time friend in the Secret Service, someone he could trust since it was starting to seem like no one on the inside could be trusted.

An hour later, Tony met up with his good friend, Mark Wallace, a forty-two-year-old agent that had seen a lot in the government, which he had been protecting for over ten years. He had a medium build and stood foot even. He was well groomed and wore a military haircut and was clean shaven.

"Mark, how's the president's behavior been since the California thing?"

"He's been asking a lot about what they're saying while in custody. He also asked if they had bail or if they'd be released. Why do you ask, Tony?"

"The call I had before I came over here was with Director Davenport of the bureau. He informed me of some things I needed to relay to the president. However, another call came in and said that the president would not care about what I had to say to him and not to relay the info."

He continued on about the possible connections between those in California and Rakman Hussein. It all made sense; however, it sounded crazy to fresh ears finding out about this.

"Calm down, Tony. We can figure this thing out

together. We have to be smart about this."

Mark continued to give Tony his views and layout of how they would continue pursuing this.

Meanwhile back in Harrisburg, Agent Miles and his family were sitting down for a soul-food dinner that Deborah had made with love.

He was enjoying the family time after knowing that he had made his point by giving information to the media, spreading and exposing the truth of the men behind the escape of Rakman.

"I can't believe how our government does so much to cover up its secrets and alliances with those most would frown upon."

"It's okay, honey, you did the right thing protecting and serving, as you took an oath to do so," Deborah said, looking on at him with loving eyes.

Agent Miles smiled when he saw the love and appreciation in her eyes and smile.

Something made him halt the conversation as he

turned his ear to the front door as if he heard something or someone outside. He knew the bureau had placed twenty-four-hour surveillance outside his home, with counter-surveillance watching them as well, just in case something went wrong as it did before.

He put his finger up to indicate silence as he made his way to the front door to see if anything seemed out of place or worth being on alert.

As soon as he opened the front door his heart began pounding as a wave of fear came over him upon seeing all of the agents slumped over in their vehicles in front of his house. Even the counter-surveillance truck agents were all unconscious in their vehicles. He reacted by slamming the door as he prepared to run to get his gun. However, when he turned around, he was met by two men in fatigues, holding guns to his wife's and daughter's heads.

"You can kill me! Just don't hurt my family," Agent Miles pleaded, not realizing that these men had not come to negotiate.

"Agent Miles, do you have someone you can call to pick up your daughter?" one of the men asked.

Hearing this statement made him realize that he could not talk or plead his way out of the situation. He and his wife would die today. For better or for worse, this was the end. Agent Miles nervously shook his head as his eyes watered. He knew that death was just moments away.

"My wife!" his voice broke in emotional pain. "Please leave her. She's not the problem. I'll suffer, not her."

However, these men came to do a job and terminate anyone who appeared to be a threat to expose the men behind Rakman and the agencies.

"You should have thought about your family a long time ago. Now is not the time," the operative said, allowing the agent's daughter to run to him.

As soon as she jumped into his embrace, the two

operatives contained the scene and killed his wife with a silenced round. She dropped where she stood. This was followed by multiple rounds that hit Agent Miles, killing him and hitting his daughter who he was hugging. The operatives staged the house as planned before calling 911 and reporting shots fired.

Within minutes, multiple Harrisburg police officers were on the scene, where they found the downed agents in their vehicles, followed by the side door of Agent Miles's home wide open. The officers radioed for backup when they saw the open door. The other officers moved in on the door with their guns out. They could see the door had been breached by force since the wood frame was cracked. Fingers rested up against the triggers as they entered with caution, only to be greeted with Agent Miles's and his wife's bloody bodies. The officers moved inside and saw the little girl. After one of them checked her pulse, she opened her eyes in fear.

"She's alive! Get a medic, stat!" the officer yelled out. "Who could do this to a child?" the officer vented, becoming emotional since he had a daughter of his own.

"You're going to be all right, sweetie," a female officer said as she caressed the little girl's hair.

She saw that the girl also had been hit by a slug in the back. The female officer started to cry, because she had a boy and a girl of her own.

"Don't be scared, baby girl, you're safe now."

The little girl blinked, and a tear slid down her face. It was obvious that she knew that the bad men had taken her mommy and daddy away.

It didn't take long for medical attention to arrive and stabilize the young girl. The Feds also came after an officer called it in. Each of the agents became emotional upon seeing the downed Agent Miles and his wife. The FBI agents took control over the scene as well as secured Miles's daughter with multiple agents.

"Gentlemen, we appreciate your securing this crime scene; however, due to national security, this case and scene will be taken over by the bureau," the lead agent said to the Harrisburg Police, wanting them to keep a tight lip.

Director Davenport was at home when he received a call informing him of the massacre of his agent and the agent's wife. He took it hard and broke down emotionally. He then ordered the agents in Harrisburg to make the situation public, but he left out the part where they staged the house to look like it was a drug deal gone bad.

After the call, he put his hands to his face. He wanted to emotionally escape the pain he was feeling from the abrupt loss of his agent.

"How many more people have to be killed before the truth is exposed?" Director Davenport said to himself.

He was angry and torn, and he wanted to get resolve without costing anyone else their life.

CHAPTER 14

RAKMAN MANAGED TO sneak into the country at 9:05 p.m. and make his way over to his first wife's house in El Paso. As always she embraced his presence, since she had not seen him in some time, yet she maintained her loyalty knowing who he was and having love for him.

"Afeni, I'm going to be around a little while this time. When I leave, we're going back to Saudi Arabia to embrace our culture more."

"It sounds promising, Rakman. I just hope you come back whenever you leave this house, so we can be a family. I do enjoy seeing you every day," she said.

Rakman and his wife continued to bond over new information and old memories. He then made his way out to the garage where his artillery was located. His grenades, rifles, and handguns were all stored in the workshop cabinets.

~ ~ ~

At 10:10 p.m. Tommy started to call all of the numbers of Nino's crew that were provided to him by the agencies.

"Who's this?"

"This is Mike, Ramon's replacement, and Nino's new line. We have to link up so we can get shit worked out with the product and the 2.4 he owes me and my associates. I know about you and the other nigga, Pistol."

"Since you're aware, then you know he got bagged by the Feds last night."

"The Feds let him go for his cooperation. He no longer exists, since he was dealt with. As for your boy Dollar, the Feds killed him in a shootout."

"Damn, folk, they put my nigga down?" L-Geez said, thinking about Dollar not being able to get away as he did.

"I need to get at you and your boy, Pistol, ASAP!"

"Where do you want to meet us?"

"I'll come to you in Miami. I'll fly down tonight, and we can handle BI in the morning."

"Say no more, folk. We here!" L-Geez said before hanging up the phone and turning to Pistol. "Aye, that nigga Nino is dead. He ratted on somebody, but this new nigga on some rich shit knows we down here and all of our names and shit. Yo, pour some of the Henny out for Dollar. The Feds killed him, the rich nigga said on the phone," L-Geez explained, haunted by the thought of his homie being gunned down.

Tommy Guns then hit up Tre and put him on point with him having to link up with the North Carolina niggas in his hood.

CHAPTER 15

AT 9:11 THE next morning in California, Governor Rendell and Senator Caine were being released after cooperating with the Feds. The press was in front of the Federal holding center awaiting their exit.

"Here they come!" a reporter yelled out, alerting everyone as they came out. "Governor Rendell, why did they release you if you helped a known terrorist escape custody?"

"Senator Caine! What role did you play in all of this?"

"Governor Rendell! We lost Federal agents trying to cover up your secrets. How do you feel about this, sir?"

Questions flew from every angle as they tried to ignore as many as of them as they could while being escorted to their awaiting vehicles.

"I told the FBI what I knew. I didn't sell out my country! I did the right thing to save my country!" Governor Rendell responded with anger as they rushed him to his car to make a getaway from the reporters.

Senator Caine tried to act if he was innocent, but the reporters did not buy it. They rushed him off as well, allowing him to evade any more questions that would expose the truth even more.

~ ~ ~

Ra Ra was having brunch at 10:16 in Mexico with his beautiful wife, Carmen; her Uncle Hector; and the directors of the NSA, CIA, and CTD. They were all enjoying the food, but that was not the reason that they had all gathered.

"Gentlemen, I see you all don't have things under control with the governor and senator. They have been exposed, and I do not want this leading back to my home," Hector announced with a calm yet assertive power.

"Hector, we can't just kill them off or cut their heads off like we're in Juarez. It is American, remember?" the CIA DO said.

"You don't have to do a thing. I have *mi familia* right here who can take care of this for us," Hector responded, pointing at Ra Ra, who had been trained by the men at the table. He learned quickly and was already very comfortable with the all the weapons. "If you gentlemen don't resolve this soon, it's going to backfire. Rakman has become a great liability to what we have. I asked him to come to my country for this meeting, but he did not show. We need to figure out what to do with him and the men in your government before we can no longer contain the situation."

As a man of power and resources, Hector had his entire compound secured with close to three hundred loyal goons of whom he took good care. Even their families were taken care of to assure that their loyalty remained with him at all times. He also knew the agency men were backed by a great power, so he, too, was always alert in case they may one day have a change of heart when it came to ending their business relationship.

"We could have Rakman brought in to appease the public and the Feds who want him?" the CTD DO suggested.

"Or we could kill him and display his death publicly, so they know he is dead and could not escape or be a threat to the nation any longer!" the NSA DO spoke up.

Ra Ra sat there eating his steak and eggs while

listening to the conversations. They were all just together months ago drinking, smoking, and talking about the good life. Now the governor, senator, and Rakman were no longer in the circle of power. All three agency heads, including Hector, came to a conclusion on what needed to be done with these men. They all had to go and be erased from the face of the earth.

"We can't forget about the other problem we have," the CIA DO said.

"How about we meet in the middle? You have your guys team up with our guys. We can handle this in a smooth and professional way," the CTD DO suggested.

"Ra Ra, do you want to work with their man?" Hector asked.

"I'm in as long as money is being made. A job is a

job. I need real money to do this. Just so y'all know, we're talking about political figures."

"I believe $10 million to have it all secured should be more than enough for you to get this done professionally," Hector responded, scanning the faces of his associates because they would have to partake in paying Ra Ra for the job.

Ra Ra smiled, mentally embracing the $10 million figure in his mind. It was certainly a sum far from what he was doing in the hood back in Atlanta.

"Mr. Smith," the CIA DO began, "we have a bonus $5 million for another job we'll discuss with you that needs to be secured."

"I'm here to get it done for the right price; and since y'all talking money, it's going to get done," Ra Ra said before taking another bite of his steak and eggs.

He then processed everything that was about to take place. But he knew he was in good hands with these government muthafuckas.

~ ~ ~

Tommy Guns met Raven, Tre, and his little homies at 11:00 a.m. at a Jamaican restaurant in downtown Miami. He put Tre onto the whole story with the nigga on the plane who wanted him to secure the money and product from the young niggas that worked for Nino.

"OG Tommy Guns, that's a lot of work, my nigga," Tre replied.

"We got this. They gave me his contacts too, so I'll be good moving it."

"You know me and my team down here in Miami got you. We can get at this paper like the old days."

Tommy laughed thinking about his words.

"We definitely got mansion money now, my

nigga," Tommy said.

Tre stood up when he saw Pistol and L-Geez walk into the restaurant.

"Yo, what's up, Pistol?"

"You know this nigga, Tre?" Tommy Guns asked.

"Yeah, he good peoples. We in business together."

Tommy greeted the two niggas and shook their hands before they sat down to get down to business.

"So who has the cocaine or 2.4 Ms?" Tommy asked.

"I got the work. We can get the money because our folks been hitting us up. We just wanted to wait to link up with you," L-Geez said.

Pistol looked at Tommy Guns and thought that he looked familiar.

"Mike, did anyone ever tell you that you look like that nigga Tommy Guns?" Pistol asked.

Tommy started laughing hard. "Nah, little nigga, I never heard that one before," he said, not feeling like it was time to let them in on what was going on.

The crew sat back and enjoyed the Jamaican meal of jerk chicken, curry goat, oxtails, rice, beans, cabbage, and a fresh salad on the side. They chased it all down with Jamaican colas. While they ate, they talked business and secured future deals.

"I want y'all to focus on locking this city and state down and to expand into Tampa, Fort Lauderdale, Jacksonville, and more. It's time to eat!" Tommy said, grooming the young squad.

Tre's cell phone sounded off, and he saw that it was Ra Ra.

"This is Ra Ra. What's up, folk?"

Tommy shook his head. "Not over the airwaves," he reminded Tre.

"You know me, I'm doing my numbers and living this life a little better by the day . . . I'll be in the States soon. I'ma stop through to holla at ya . . . See ya when ya come through, folk," Tre said before hanging up the phone. "He's coming through soon, he said. So it'll all be a good reunion," Tre said with a smile.

They finished up their food and then made their way back to their whips. As they stood talking briefly about where they were going to meet up, screeching tires and abrupt gunfire erupted and got their immediate attention. At the same time, Tre saw his homie Jay drop from slugs that tracked him down. A car full of Jamaicans with fully automatic weapons yelled and shot at them from their car windows.

"Yo, man! Him a dead man walking fo' real!"

The whole crew returned fire. They wanted to gun down the dreadlock muthafuckas with their superstitions.

"OG, you got beef with these niggas?" Tre asked.

"Nah, little nigga. Do you?"

"I don't fuck with them. They do them and I do me," Tre said in between firing rounds back at them.

"*Toma! Toma!* Die *tu cabrons!*" Raven yelled while squeezing the trigger and unleashing multiple rounds.

She killed one of the dreads and then shifted her weapons around for more action. Tommy Guns brought his twin nickel-plated .45 Desert Eagles into view and squeezed off rounds. He dropped the mother of these Jamaican niggas with chest shots that breached his vital organs and left him with no chance of survival. At the sight of him falling, the other dreadlock niggas started spraying their Uzis in Tommy Guns's direction, forcing him to take cover.

"Bumblaclot! I'll kill 'em dead fo' sure!" the Jamaican cat yelled out.

"What the fuck are they talking about?" Tre asked.

They all shot back at the Jamaican muthafuckas, with their slugs crashing into their faces and making their brains leap out the other side. It brought a halt to their gangsta shit. There was only one still standing firm until he ran out of bullets. He tried to run, but Raven popped up in front of him. She fired slugs into his chest, which thrust him back and punctured his lungs at the same time.

Although he was still breathing, she ran down on him and looked into his eyes. She was the prettiest thing he had seen in awhile. She was a natural beauty but the angel of death. She then raised her guns in view and fired off into both his eye sockets, abruptly exploding his eyes and killing him instantly.

Just when they thought it was over another car turned the corner loud and fast.

"Drive by!" L-Geez yelled out when he saw the car coming with a Jamaican nigga hanging out the window.

Everyone shifted their attention and fired toward the crazy nigga hanging out of the window with a 12-gauge shotgun, firing roaring loudly as each buckshot sprayed in their direction.

"Kill all of these muthafucking dreadlock niggas!" Tommy Guns yelled.

They focused their shots and killed the driver, which forced a loud crash that ejected the nigga from the front seat through the windshield killing him instantly.

The last Jamaican in the back seat tried to slide out of the car and run, but he knew that he was alone and outnumbered.

"Papi, he's trying to run!" Raven yelled out to Tre.

He quickly turned around and busted shots into the nigga's back, dropping him where he stood. They all ran down on him and saw that he was still alive. He wanted to know why they were shooting at them. Raven saw that he was going for his gun on his waist, until she put her foot on his hand and aimed her guns at him.

"Don't even think about it, punta!" she said, eyeing him down while ready to pull the triggers.

The Jamaican's eyes lit up as Tommy Guns came into view as if he had seen a ghost.

"Yo, bumblaclot! Him a dead man walking before ya!"

"What the fuck you talking about?" Pistol said, now also aiming his gun at him.

"Da man have many faces and lives ya don't know."

"This nigga talking that voodoo bullshit!" Tommy said.

"*Oye, viejo*, give me the word and he's dead!" Raven said standing by.

"Ya can't kill me, ya know. I'm going to always live through the earth!"

"Raven, kill this nigga!" Tommy said before he turned to Tre. "Kill this nigga and his crew twice so they don't have a chance of coming back."

Tre did just that. He killed the man and fired off multiple shots into all of their heads before leaving the crime scene and scared onlookers behind.

~ ~ ~

At 1:09 p.m. at the White House, the FBI director, Homeland Security director, and Head Secret Service agent Mark Wallace were all sitting in front of the president explaining the facts of the case. They further briefed him on what had happened with Agent Miles and his family. The president listened to the three men before him who represented the nation's best interests. He now had an obligation to resolve the matter. The president arranged a meeting with all his joint chiefs of staff to discuss the situation and to get to the bottom of it.

"Gentlemen, we don't need a war on our hands inside our own government. This is unacceptable. I will get resolve once I speak with our military's elite to see what they know of this."

"We appreciate the time you're taking, Mr. President. These agents and their families need closure from this horrifying ordeal."

CHAPTER 16

AT 7:02 P.M. the president was in the West Wing meeting with all of the military heads to discuss the matter.

"Gentlemen, from what has been brought to my attention regarding the four agents and one agent's family, the men doing this are trained elites from within our government. I would like to know if any of your men have taken part in this?"

The men all shook their heads no.

"From my knowledge, none of my men were involved," marine four-star General Thompson replied.

"We need to resolve this situation. We cannot have our own government killing off Federal agents. It's political genocide. The CIA and other agencies may be responsible for these rogue acts. I want answers, men, and I needed them yesterday."

"Yes, sir, Mr. President," they all chimed in, standing and saluting the president as he exited the room.

The joint military generals and admiral all knew they needed to assemble an elite group of soldiers to contain this problem that had reached the White House. They informed their men about the level of seriousness and who their targets could be. The marines, navy, air force, and army all brought together their best men to form the Elite Force. The group met at an undisclosed location for a mission and weapons check, where they all received their tactical gear together.

Meanwhile back at the White House, the president was sitting in the study watching the flames in the fireplace as thoughts of what had taken place filled his mind. He knew he could not afford to allow this to continue. The president also thought about how American voters would frown upon how close he was with powerful people, and especially at how he used to laugh with the men who brought Rakman into play to create his plots of terror. He could not afford to be exposed, so he felt it was best that all those involved be silenced forever, because no one was going to jeopardize his position of absolute power.

CHAPTER 17

SENATOR CAINE WAS enjoying dinner with a female associate at 6:09 at the sidewalk cafe under the umbrella, which shielded them from the California sun.

"Sir, would you care for another glass of wine?" the waiter said as he walked up to their table.

"Um, I think I'll go for something a little stronger this time around. Let me get a double shot of Jack Daniels on the rocks."

"Yes, sir. Anything for the lady?"

"Bring her another glass of red wine, please."

The waiter walked away, leaving the senator to discuss with his female associate about the scheme behind the agents being killed and what he knew of the men on the inside of the unfolding conspiracy. Instinct made him halt the conversation as he started looking around. He felt as if he was being watched—and he was. He took notice of a Crown Victoria parked across the street with a microphone pointed in his direction listening to their conversation. His heart started beating fast as he feared the worst. What's going to happen? he thought, trying not to panic.

He turned back to his lady friend wanting to alert her, since he did not know how long they had been watched or how much information they had gathered listening to him. The men in the car did not know that they had been seen. The senator continued on as if they were not there.

"Here are your drinks. Jack for the gentleman and red wine for the lady," the waiter said when he appeared.

"Young man, can I see your pen for a second?" the

senator asked.

"Yes, sir. Here you go."

The senator wrote on a napkin about the men across the street.

"Young man, you're a good waiter. What's your name?"

"Ray, sir."

"Nice job, Ray. Interesting accent, too," he said, creating small talk since his nerves were getting the best of him.

"My accent is from Georgia, sir."

"Well, Ray, I'm going to make sure I leave you a nice tip and let the owner here know that you're an asset to their business."

The waiter walked away, leaving them to continue with their meal. Senator Caine then picked up his glass of Jack.

"This is for the road and exposing the truth," he said before quickly drinking the double shot and feeling its warmth go down. "Ahh, the warm feeling of Jack going down. There's nothing like it."

"The wine is great, too. I'll pay for dinner to take some of the stress off of you," the reporter said.

"No, no! I insist on covering this bill," he responded as he reached into his pocket for his wallet.

The waiter returned and saw that their evening was winding down.

"How were your meal and drinks? Was everything to your liking?"

"Yes! We're just ready to pay and leave. Something came up."

The waiter handed the senator the leather checkbook with the bill enclosed for privacy. At the same time, the senator reached for his heart. He felt a constricting yet sharp pain burn in his chest. His eyes widened, fearing death was on its way. He struggled to hold on as the sharp pain took over his body. The reporter screamed for help, adding to his fear that something had gone terribly wrong. He fell from the chair heaving that he wanted to live and wanted to say more. However, his end was now. His body shook violently before coming to a rest as life escaped his flesh.

The agencies had sent Ra Ra to take the senator out. They knew he frequented the restaurant, so tainting his drink with a chemical compound that induced a heart attack was an easy way to take him out.

Ra Ra calmly walked away when the agents in the car across the street saw him slide off to the side street of the restaurant. They realized that his actions were not something an employee would do in the middle of a man having a heart attack.

"Hey! Stop right there!" the agents yelled out, running after Ra Ra.

Ra Ra could not afford to be compromised, so he stopped running and turned around. He swiftly fired off silenced rounds that dropped the two agents who were pursuing him, stopping them dead in their tracks. He did not stick around to see if they were alive. Ra Ra took off running until he was picked up by a driver sent from the agencies.

CHAPTER 18

IN EL PASO, Tommy Guns was dressed as a Muslim in full garb and kufi when he knocked on Rakman's wife's door with his .44 Magnum concealed ready to take him out. His daughter came to the door.

"Can I help you?"

"As-salamu alaykum, sister. My name is McMum A Shukar. I'm wondering if your father is home."

It was strange to her since no one ever came to their house asking for her father.

"He is not, but can I take a message?" she asked, wanting to know more about the man standing at their door.

"Let him know a good friend from Harrisburg, Pennsylvania, stopped by."

She nodded her head and looked at him as she

closed the door. He turned around and walked back toward his car that was parked blocks away. At the same time, he paid attention to all the passing cars. He spotted Rakman in a gold Lexus LS600. In his adrenaline-filled excitement, he fired off multiple shots at the passing car, with slugs slamming into the frame and alerting Rakman of the oncoming bullets.

Rakman quickly turned to see who was firing on him, and in that very instant, he made eye contact with Tommy Guns, who he thought was dead just like the rest of the nation did. He raced off in his car knowing he could not return to the house anytime soon. So, he figured he would lay low and out of sight.

Tommy ran toward his car, knowing that the police would be on the scene fast. He mashed the gas to get away from the area thinking about how bad he wanted to kill this muthafucka.

~ ~ ~

California Governor Rendell was at his home in a gated community gathering papers to be mailed out to protect himself over the unfolding schemes. He knew what had taken place with Senator Caine and the agents who were shot when they chased a suspect. He knew it was just a matter of time before someone came for him. It was inevitable, which is why he ordered more security to prevent what he could.

At 8:15 p.m., a black minivan pulled into the community in front of the governor's home, blasting music and disturbing the quiet residents. Security immediately approached the van with guns in hand and told the driver to move. As soon as the security closed in on the van, it took off and raced out of the community. It was the perfect distraction for the two assassins to enter the mansion, where they swept

183

through each room and took out all security guards and staff members.

Once all the rooms had been secured, they made their way into the governor's study. In the moment he saw the two men before him, he knew the end was mere seconds away.

"This isn't personal, sir. It's simply a job," the man said, knowing the governor knew exactly who they were.

They cleared his desk of the paperwork and letters he was attempting to mail out to all the media outlets. They then forced him to write a suicide note before they handed him a gun with one bullet in it.

"Take the gun, sir. You already know what to do with it."

Each of the trained men had their silenced weapons pointed at him in case he wanted to shift the gun. He nervously held the gun while shaking and crying as he placed it to his temple with his finger resting on the trigger. He realized that the compromised situation he was in was fucked up. Even if he tried to shift his weapon, he would only get off one shot. He knew he could not kill himself, so he set down the gun.

Immediately, Ra Ra pumped a silenced round into the governor's temple before taking the other gun and firing it out the window to alert the security. He then placed the gun back into the governor's hand before the two men made their escape and left the scene. By the time the guards had woken up, the governor was dead from an apparent suicide.

CHAPTER 19

CTA DIRECTOR PRICE was fast asleep at his home in Lincoln, Nebraska, at 10:02 p.m. when he heard his dogs barking wildly as if someone was in his home. Being in the field and knowing the line of business he was in made him paranoid and alert. He immediately grabbed his 9mm from the nightstand and got out of bed to see what was going on. He moved quietly toward the bedroom door. However, he did not know the Elite Force was already in his home, some of them already in the bedroom standing behind him.

One of the agents fired silenced tranquilizer darts into his sleeping wife to keep her down, and then one into the director's back that dropped him where he stood. They staged his body, tying a rope around his neck and then securing him to the balcony overlooking the living room. They then tossed him over, snapping his neck from the abrupt force of his falling body, which killed him instantly and made his death appear to be a suicide. He never had a chance against the trained group of men and their skill set to take out and contain all targets. Before they left, they set a forged handwritten suicide note beneath his body.

~ ~ ~

The DO of the NSA was also sleeping in his home at 12:01 a.m., until he was awakened by the feeling of a cold barrel pressed up against his face from the silenced MK5. As he opened his eyes, he zoomed in on all of the men in fatigues, the night-vision goggles, and the silenced weapons. He did not question how they got past his security system, because it was America's finest before him. They hit him with a tranquilizer dart before injecting his arm with a high dose of raw uncut heroin. The hot shot raced through his body. His heart sped up and gave him the greatest feeling of euphoric sensation before it stopped, and a gasp of air released as he was no more.

~ ~ ~

The CTD director was in his car at 8:02 a.m. on his way to work when he smelled something burning. His attention then shifted toward the vents where he saw sparks coming from them followed by flames. Instinctively, he tried to put out the fire himself, but to no avail, so he slammed his foot on the brake to get control of the car. However, the brakes were not working. His heart and mind raced as he tried not to panic in his unwieldy situation. His car was going over sixty-five miles per hour. He was unable to stop while he was locked inside his car that was on fire.

"No! No! This can't be happening!" he yelled out

in fear of dying by way of a fiery death.

The airbags suddenly burst out of the steering wheel and passenger side, which knocked him unconscious and caused his car to drive out of control. It swayed toward the guard railing and flipped over the bridge into the water, killing him on impact by snapping his back.

~ ~ ~

At 11:04 p.m. while the Elite Force tracked down Rakman, Ra Ra was moving in on his target in Miami. He entered the lavish resort where his target had been staying for the last few days. He made his way up to the penthouse suite with his silenced 9mms. He moved discreetly through the lavish suite that boasted well-appointed bedrooms, a dining room, a living room area, a fully stocked bar, and a 60-inch-screen TV. Ra Ra could hear the television in the bedroom with females in the room talking. Then it happened.

"You come into my suite thinking you're going to take me out, huh?" Tommy Guns said with his gun pointing at the nigga in all black. "Turn around, nigga."

Ra Ra turned around and saw the face of Tommy Guns, but he did not recognize him since he had changed his look when Tony was alive.

"You don't even know who I am, do you?"

"I came here to deal with Mike Mitchell. If you're not him, then I got the wrong room."

Tommy lowered his gun and broke into a smile.

"Ra Ra, you stupid little nigga. It's me, Tommy Guns."

It took a few seconds for him to really look. He then could tell that it was really him.

"My nigga, Tommy Guns. I thought you were

dead!" Ra Ra said, tucking his weapon to embrace his old head. "How the fuck you pull that off?" he asked.

"It's a long story. I'll put you onto it later."

"I killed that nigga Tony thinking he put a hit out on you. He had your BM and her mom killed for ratting you out."

"This shit is bigger than me!"

"I already know from my end that shit was going crazy behind the scenes. If only niggas knew," Ra Ra said, not knowing they were both connected to the same people that did not tell them this. "Yo, Tre know you around?"

"Yeah, we linked up a few times. I was sitting there when you called, but I didn't want him to tell you over the phone. These muthafuckas got me sitting on fifteen tons, Ra Ra."

Ra Ra shook his head. He now knew where that

shit came from, because he sat alongside the major players, including Hector Guzman.

"I'm glad you're back in play, Tommy. Now we're going to take this world by storm!" Ra Ra said.

"We're definitely going to get it done with the people behind me and whoever it is you got down with in Mexico."

CHAPTER 20

A FEW HOURS later, Tommy Guns, Tre, Pistol, Ra Ra, Raven, and L-Geez were all chilling at Tre's crib.

"Ra Ra, call your sister. She said she hasn't heard from you in awhile," Tommy Guns said.

"You stopped by to see her?"

"Yeah, she knows I'm around. You should have seen the look on her face."

"She loves you. You know that, right?"

"I made it official with her that she's mine. I ain't going nowhere."

Ra Ra called Candy, and she was very happy to hear from him, especially knowing he was with Tommy Guns. She felt good that they were together. They were the two men she cared about in her life, next to her son. Ra Ra hung up the phone after letting his sister know he would see her soon.

"Yo, my sis said she loves you, nigga, and hopes to see you soon. We should go to ATL and hit up 122 or Strokers," Ra Ra suggested.

"I'm down with that!" Tre said.

"We can do that and then go see ya sister together. She'll be happy to see us rolling up all thugged out."

As they prepared to head to Atlanta, the Elite Force had found Rakman hiding in Reno, the Biggest Little City in the world. He was laying low in a motel. It was the same place where he contacted his wife and Hector Guzman, which allowed the agencies to track his call back to the motel. Once the Elite Force confirmed his presence, they called back to their superiors to see if they wanted him dead or alive.

~ ~ ~

By noon, photos of the senator, governor, CIA

director, CTD director, and NSA director were plastered all over the television and media outlets. Social media outlets had hashtagged conspiracies about all these men being taken out within a twenty-four-hour period. Rakman saw this on his phone as well as on the news. He knew that his time was almost up, since all of his associates had been taken out back-to-back. This was not good. He knew that whoever it was taking them out was coming for him, so he needed to get out of the country. He decided to head back to Saudi Arabia, where he would at least have a chance to live in hiding.

But Rakman did not know that his time was coming to an end, much sooner than he had thought, until he saw a shadow pass by his room window. He got up from the bed and raced to the window to peek out. As he looked out, a concussion grenade crashed through the window. It was followed by a loud bang and a flash of brightness that disoriented him enough for them to breach the room with their weapons. Rakman did not care. He was ready to die rather than be taken in. He knew he was cornered, so he brought the grenades into view that he was holding in both hands. He was prepared to use his mouth to pull out the pins.

In that same instance, the trained Elite Force fired off multiple accurate rounds that pierced his heart and made it erupt inside of him, killing him and dropping him where he stood. They closed in quickly, flipped over his body, and took digital pictures, which they sent back to their superiors before exiting the scene and heading to their next mission.

Having six men from each branch of the military trained as they were working in sync, this team could take out a small army together and not be seen.

The Elite Force traveled to Juarez, Mexico, and found Hector Guzman's compound. They spread out to survey his soldiers around the compound. They wanted to see how alert they were, since all the other government heads had been taken out on the president's top-secret orders. Hector had seen the same news that everyone else had, so he, too, became fully alert and layered himself with soldiers to protect him at any cost.

Hector sat watching TV with his M60 machine gun at his side. He was ready to go to war. Being paranoid did not help as he nervously waited for what was to come.

"Them Americanos can never be trusted! Fucking *pendejos!*" Hector said while sitting watching TV.

Hector did not even want to go to sleep, knowing

everything that had taken place. He started sniffing his own product, something he would kill others for if he caught them doing, but his nerves and fear of falling to sleep were getting the best of him. However, the cocaine only added to his paranoia.

Outside of the compound the Elite Force blended into the grassy areas and brush as they watched all movement around the compound. They strategically waited to attack and take out their intended target, Hector Guzman.

CHAPTER 21

DARKNESS AND SILENCE fell on the compound at 10:01
p.m. Many of the Mexican soldiers were tired and had
dozed off when they should have been wide awake.
Some of them were tired from standing all day, so they
took turns sleeping. The Elite Force noted this and
moved in furtively, killing all of the sleeping soldiers
with silenced rounds. They took out multiple sleeping
Mexicans as well as those sitting around, until one
spotted his buddy failing from a headshot.

"Attack! The Americanos are here!" the man
yelled before they caught slugs in their mouths and
faces, killing him where he stood.

Loud gunfire erupted from the Mexicans' AK-47s
trying to locate where the Elite Force was hiding. They
were unaware that the muzzle flash allowed the Elite

Force members to take them out one by one as they were hidden by the darkness of the night. Inside the house, Hector Guzman placed both of his .45 automatics in his waistline before taking hold of his M60 machine gun. He was ready for war.

"*Mira!* Kill everybody shooting at us!" Hector yelled out to his men.

He took hold of his phone and called the president of the United States. He knew he was the one that authorized the attack on him. As soon as the president answered the phone, Hector snapped.

"You greedy piece of shit! We all made you rich, and this is how you repay us!"

The president calmly responded, knowing he was in control and had the absolute power.

"I'm sorry, Hector. I have no idea what you're talking about. Whatever happens to you, you brought on yourself."

"You want it all, huh? You greedy cabron! My

men are going to take out all of your men, and then I'll come to America personally to blow your brains out!"

"You'll never make it through the night, Hector," the president calmly responded before hanging up and leaving him with that taunting thought.

Hector heard his men shooting outside, so he grabbed the M60 and ran out the front door. He sprayed the weapon until his body was thrust backward, forcing him to drop the gun as the burning slugs ate at his flesh. He was so pumped up and high from snorting cocaine that he jumped up and pulled out his .45 automatic. He fired recklessly until he felt more slugs crash into his flesh, forcing him back down for good and taking his life. The Elite Force's mission was now complete. They returned to America unharmed after securing the job at hand with skill and precision.

~ ~ ~

Tommy Guns and his little homies were still

partying the night away at 1:07 a.m. He did not know that he had inherited all the money from the agencies that once belonged to Ramon. Now his only mission was to get rid of the tons of cocaine and relocate for good. For Tommy, this corrupt life had finally paid off.

~ ~ ~

The president addressed the nation at 11:00 a.m. about the matters surrounding Rakman and the men involved with him. He also made the nation aware that all the agents died in the line of duty, so they did not die in vain. America had prevailed in the end from all the corruption. He made a promise to the American people to keep the country safe from terror as well as to clean up the streets from the drugs that plagued them. All he was doing was saving face until the next multimillion-dollar deal came through from which he would benefit.

CHAPTER 22

A FEW MONTHS had passed by as the summer months closed in. Tommy Guns and his crew were on his brand-new $10 million seventy-foot yacht in the Bahamas. He also invited a few females for the homies that were single. They were all standing around drinking as the yacht parted the aqua-blue waters.

"This is the good life right here. From the hood to this big-ass yacht," Tre said while pouring liquor overboard for the homies that could not be here. "To my niggas, Geez and Little D!" he toasted.

"Yeah, to my niggas!" Ra Ra added.

"One more thing, y'all. Let's toast to my sexy lady, Raven, because I'm going to marry her when we get back to the States," Tre said before kissing his woman. Her eyes lit up with love.

"I respect that, little homie," Tommy said, eyeing the five-carat diamond set in white gold that Tre pulled out to make his ghetto proposal official.

"Raven, I love you 'til the wheels fall off, mami, and we going to do this until the end," he said, sliding the ring onto her finger.

She embraced him with love and tears in her eyes full of happiness, before pulling away from the kiss.

"Papi, I love you and, yes, 'til the wheels fall off. I'm going to give it to you good tonight, papi!" Raven said, making everybody laugh.

Candy looked at Tommy Guns and wondered where her ring was as she looked down at her finger.

"Don't worry about it; our time is coming," Tommy said to her, kissing her soft lips and making her heart smile.

"Tre, that's a nice ring you got her, too," Candy

said. "You did a good job. Raven, when we get back to the States, we going to look for dresses," Candy said, excited.

She knew that it would also give her a chance to see what type of dress she would look good in when Tommy finally asked her the big question.

Raven lit up thinking about being newly engaged. Everyone enjoyed themselves, partying until the couples found their rooms on the mega yacht. Tommy and Candy were in the master suite, where they watched TV after a long round of intimate passion. He was jotting down things in his notebook.

"What you writing, baby?" she asked.

"Some thoughts I have on the life I've lived and on the one I'm still living."

"Put that pen and paper down, because I want more of you."

He glanced over at her sexy naked body and her smooth curves that he had his hands on not too long before. He set the paper and pen down and gave her some attention. He kissed and caressed her soft body, making her heart and body smile as his fingers found their way to the place of pleasure that was warm, tight, and wet.

"Mmmmh, I love this!"

As the moment of passion heated up, a sound that he thought he was far away from brought an abrupt stop to the passion. Gunfire could be heard outside. He quickly jumped up and grabbed his faithful .44 Magnum and rushed out to the deck to see what was going on. He immediately saw men climbing onto his yacht when he looked over the side. He then introduced their faces to his .44 Magnum, killing them and spewing their brains and blood into the water, allowing them to become shark food.

Tre, Pistol, and Ra Ra were engaged in a gunfight at the front of the yacht as the men from the agencies tried to make their way onto it. Tommy still had an unresolved debt that they had tracked down after the directors of the agencies were killed. A few hundred million dollars does not just go unnoticed. Tommy Guns came up from behind the men at the front of the yacht and began shooting out with his team. They were busting shots into their heads, one by one. The fight came to a halt when they saw no more operatives.

Then a loud scream came through the air.

"Aaaaghh, Tre!"

It was Raven being held by one of the operatives who had placed a gun to her head.

"You crazy nigga! You hurt her and I'll kill you over and over!"

Tommy saw the face of the man standing there holding Raven. It was the muthafucka from the plane.

"Mr. Anderson, I told you before on the plane you have a debt of $230 million now. There's always going to be someone like me who collects no matter who dies off," he explained.

However, it was not true. He wanted the money for himself, so he sacrificed the lives of those men to appease his greed.

"Mr. Anderson, if you settle your debt, we can all go on living our lives."

"I got ya muthafucking money, but if you hurt her, you won't even get a chance to think about spending it!"

"As you know, for insurance purposes, I can't just let her go now. She'll come with me until I'm far enough from your yacht. Then if she wants to swim and become shark bait, that's on her," the man said, looking to the side of the yacht to see if his tender was floating alongside.

"I can't let you take her anywhere!" Tre snapped, ready to gun down the nigga for having his gun at Raven's head.

"Papi, I love you 'til the wheels fall off!" Raven said, sensing the end was near if he took her off the yacht.

The man feared Tre's fast approach, so he decided to shift his weapon and aimed it at Tre. Then it happened. A loud roaring of the gun erupted, startling everyone until they saw the man's face crack open from being shot in the back of the head.

Candy came out of her room and used the .32 automatic that Tommy got for her safety. She never thought she would have to use it until now. She stood there shaking since firing a gun was not her thing, but she did not want anyone bringing harm to her new friend, Raven.

Tommy ran over to her and took the gun out of her hands. He then embraced her and told her everything was going to be okay.

"You did what needed to be done, baby. Don't worry about that muthafucka; he deserved to die," Tommy Guns said before turning to his little homies. "Get these muthafuckas' bodies off my boat. The sharks are hungry."

They immediately tossed all of the bodies off the boat and into the sea, feeding them to the sharks and other sea creatures that had a taste for blood.

Tre ran up and embraced Raven with love as a thug tear came to his eye when he thought about losing the best thing that ever happened to him. She also cried at how close she had been to being taken away from the man who she loved with her all.

"You know I'm never going to leave your side, papi. I don't ever want to be too far away from this dick!" she said, trying to be funny and make light of the situation. "But for real, I love you and appreciate what you mean to me and have done for me, papi," she said, kissing him as she held onto him with love and passion.

Tommy was also in the moment with his girl, Candy, before shifting his focus to make sure his staff kept their mouths shut. He paid them well to do so. The entire crew stayed up drinking while at the same time appreciating the life they had.

~ ~ ~

Two months later, Tommy Guns, Candy, his mother, and his three sons were all at his multimillion-dollar mansion along the coast in Mexico. He made sure his crew back in the United States was set up financially for life. He had a couple hundred million dollars that would last a lifetime. Selling drugs for him was out of the question now, unless he had to make a move.

He also managed to marry Candy and make her Mrs. Anderson, something she always wanted to be from the beginning of their relationship. Now they lived a normal life away from the streets, yet an affluent lifestyle that was well deserved.

Tommy Guns was now writing about the life he lived up to this point and the people he encountered along the way. He knew most people would not believe how it had all unfolded. The others certainly would not want him to tell everything that had happened. So when he put his book out, he titled it

Corrupt City and labeled it a fiction story with real-life events.

At the end of his book, he quoted, "The truth is all how you perceive it!"

Text Good2Go at 31996 to receive new release updates via text message.

To order books, please fill out the order form below:
To order films please go to www.good2gofilms.com

Name: ___ _____

Address:_____

City: _____ State: _____ Zip Code: _____

Phone:_____

Email:_____

Method of Payment: Check   VISA   MASTERCARD

Credit Card#:_ _____

Name as it appears on card: _____

Signature: _____

Item Name	Price	Qty	Amount
48 Hours to Die – Silk White	$14.99		
A Hustler's Dream - Ernest Morris	$14.99		
A Hustler's Dream 2 - Ernest Morris	$14.99		
A Thug's Devotion – J. L. Rose and J. M. McMillon	$14.99		
All Eyes on Tommy Gunz – Warren Holloway	$14.99		
All Eyes on Tommy Gunz 2 – Warren Holloway	$14.99		
All Eyes on Tommy Gunz 3 – Warren Holloway	$14.99		
All Eyes on Tommy Gunz 4 – Warren Holloway	$14.99		
Black Reign – Ernest Morris	$14.99		
Bloody Mayhem Down South – Trayvon Jackson	$14.99		
Bloody Mayhem Down South 2 – Trayvon Jackson	$14.99		
Business Is Business – Silk White	$14.99		
Business Is Business 2 – Silk White	$14.99		
Business Is Business 3 – Silk White	$14.99		
Childhood Sweethearts – Jacob Spears	$14.99		
Childhood Sweethearts 2 – Jacob Spears	$14.99		
Childhood Sweethearts 3 - Jacob Spears	$14.99		
Childhood Sweethearts 4 - Jacob Spears	$14.99		
Connected To The Plug – Dwan Marquis Williams	$14.99		
Connected To The Plug 2 – Dwan Marquis Williams	$14.99		
Connected To The Plug 3 – Dwan Williams	$14.99		
Deadly Reunion – Ernest Morris	$14.99		
Dream's Life – Assa Raymond Baker	$14.99		
Flipping Numbers – Ernest Morris	$14.99		
Flipping Numbers 2 – Ernest Morris	$14.99		
He Loves Me, He Loves You Not - Mychea	$14.99		

He Loves Me, He Loves You Not 2 - Mychea	$14.99		
He Loves Me, He Loves You Not 3 - Mychea	$14.99		
He Loves Me, He Loves You Not 4 – Mychea	$14.99		
He Loves Me, He Loves You Not 5 – Mychea	$14.99		
Lord of My Land – Jay Morrison	$14.99		
Lost and Turned Out – Ernest Morris	$14.99		
Love Hates Violence – De'Wayne Maris	$14.99		
Married To Da Streets – Silk White	$14.99		
M.E.R.C. - Make Every Rep Count Health and Fitness	$14.99		
Money Make Me Cum – Ernest Morris	$14.99		
My Besties – Asia Hill	$14.99		
My Besties 2 – Asia Hill	$14.99		
My Besties 3 – Asia Hill	$14.99		
My Besties 4 – Asia Hill	$14.99		
My Boyfriend's Wife - Mychea	$14.99		
My Boyfriend's Wife 2 – Mychea	$14.99		
My Brothers Envy – J. L. Rose	$14.99		
My Brothers Envy 2 – J. L. Rose	$14.99		
Naughty Housewives – Ernest Morris	$14.99		
Naughty Housewives 2 – Ernest Morris	$14.99		
Naughty Housewives 3 – Ernest Morris	$14.99		
Naughty Housewives 4 – Ernest Morris	$14.99		
Never Be The Same – Silk White	$14.99		
Shades of Revenge – Assa Raymond Baker	$14.99		
Slumped – Jason Brent	$14.99		
Someone's Gonna Get It – Mychea	$14.99		
Stranded – Silk White	$14.99		
Supreme & Justice – Ernest Morris	$14.99		
Supreme & Justice 2 – Ernest Morris	$14.99		
Supreme & Justice 3 – Ernest Morris	$14.99		
Tears of a Hustler - Silk White	$14.99		
Tears of a Hustler 2 - Silk White	$14.99		
Tears of a Hustler 3 - Silk White	$14.99		

Tears of a Hustler 4- Silk White	$14.99		
Tears of a Hustler 5 – Silk White	$14.99		
Tears of a Hustler 6 – Silk White	$14.99		
The Panty Ripper - Reality Way	$14.99		
The Panty Ripper 3 – Reality Way	$14.99		
The Solution – Jay Morrison	$14.99		
The Teflon Queen – Silk White	$14.99		
The Teflon Queen 2 – Silk White	$14.99		
The Teflon Queen 3 – Silk White	$14.99		
The Teflon Queen 4 – Silk White	$14.99		
The Teflon Queen 5 – Silk White	$14.99		
The Teflon Queen 6 - Silk White	$14.99		
The Vacation – Silk White	$14.99		
Tied To A Boss - J.L. Rose	$14.99		
Tied To A Boss 2 - J.L. Rose	$14.99		
Tied To A Boss 3 - J.L. Rose	$14.99		
Tied To A Boss 4 - J.L. Rose	$14.99		
Tied To A Boss 5 - J.L. Rose	$14.99		
Time Is Money - Silk White	$14.99		
Tomorrow's Not Promised – Robert Torres	$14.99		
Tomorrow's Not Promised 2 – Robert Torres	$14.99		
Two Mask One Heart – Jacob Spears and Trayvon Jackson	$14.99		
Two Mask One Heart 2 – Jacob Spears and Trayvon Jackson	$14.99		
Two Mask One Heart 3 – Jacob Spears and Trayvon Jackson	$14.99		
Wrong Place Wrong Time – Silk White	$14.99		
Young Goonz – Reality Way	$14.99		
Subtotal:			
Tax:			
Shipping (Free) U.S. Media Mail:			
Total:			

Make Checks Payable To:
Good2Go Publishing
7311 W Glass Lane,
Laveen, AZ 85339

CPSIA information can be obtained
at www.ICGtesting.com
Printed in the USA
LVHW051523110419
613829LV00017B/642